Also by Judy Christie
and available from Center Point Large Print:

Gone to Green
Goodness Gracious Green

**This Large Print Book carries the
Seal of Approval of N.A.V.H.**

THE GLORY OF GREEN

Center Poi
Large Pri

THE GLORY OF GREEN

The Green Series

Judy Christie

CENTER POINT PUBLISHING
THORNDIKE, MAINE

This Center Point Large Print edition
is published in the year 2011 by arrangement with
Abingdon Press.

The text of this Large Print edition is unabridged.
In other aspects, this book may vary
from the original edition.
Printed in the United States of America
on permanent paper.
Set in 16-point Times New Roman type.

ISBN: 978-1-61173-151-4

Library of Congress Cataloging-in-Publication Data

Christie, Judy Pace, 1956–
The glory of green / Judy Christie. — Center Point large print ed.
p. cm.
ISBN 978-1-61173-151-4 (library binding : alk. paper)
1. Women journalists—Fiction. 2. City and town life—Louisiana—Fiction.
3. Community life—Louisiana—Fiction. 4. Large type books. I. Title.
PS3603.H7525G56 2011
813'.6—dc22

2011010820

To Paul, with love

ACKNOWLEDGMENTS

Annual Golden Pen Awards Given from *The Green News-Item* with many thanks from Lois Barker and Judy Christie

Thank you to all the wonderful readers who keep going to Green! Many supporters help Lois Barker on her journey, and deep thanks go to *The Green News-Item* community correspondents, who contribute great local news.

The most recent Golden Pen Award for outstanding reporting for the Green newspaper is shared by Melanie Pace and Virginia Disotell. Runners-up, for adding fantastic touches to the news from Green, are Carol Lovelady, Pat Lingenfelter, Annette Boyd, Karen Enriquez, Ginger Hamilton, Frances Derreck, Paul Christie, Kathie Rowell, Alan English, Craig Durrett, Mary Ann Van Osdell, and Don Walker. Fine reporters, all, keeping you up-to-date on what is happening in Green. Heartfelt thanks to each of you!

In addition, the staff thanks the newspaper supporters who went above and beyond to help with *The Glory of Green*—Kathie Rowell, Paul Christie, Pat Lingenfelter, and Mary Frances Christie, my wonderful agent Etta Wilson, and fantastic editor Barbara Scott. Lois and I could never make it without you.

THE GLORY OF GREEN

1

*A neighbor in the Ashland community wants
the hoodlums who took his U.S. flag from the
pole in the front yard and replaced it with
boxer shorts to return his flag. However, the
perpetrators should not expect to get their
shorts back. "The red hearts aren't my style,
but Martha Sue seems to like them," he told
this correspondent with a wink. If you ask
me, it's a sad day when Old Glory gets
undermined by underwear.*
—The Green News-Item

Chris Craig was so kind and fun—and good-
looking—that I could scarcely believe he would
be my husband in less than a month.

But I was having a hard time believing what he
had just said.

"Don't you think that's the perfect solution?" he
asked, a big smile on his face. "We don't need this
place, since we'll be living in your house."

My fiancé was supposed to give away his catfish
collection.

Instead, here I sat, at his kitchen table, with
woven, ceramic, and stuffed catfish everywhere.
And there he stood, drinking coffee out of a mug
with a fish handle, tossing out a suggestion that was
bigger than his heart. And Chris had a big heart.

11

"It hit me last night after I dropped you off," he said. "Those boys deserve better than that shack back behind the church. This trailer isn't worth much, but they'd have room to run and play, and the roof doesn't leak."

While Chris talked about changing lives, my thoughts strayed back to that catfish collection. Getting a husband at age thirty-eight was one thing; taking all his things was something else. My cozy cottage, with its mix of antiques and modern art, was arranged the way I liked it.

I looked around the paneled room and wondered who thought the catfish pillow on the couch had been a good idea. Just because Chris raised the whiskered fish part time didn't make him a fan of the creatures as art objects. *Did it?*

"So, what do you think?" he asked. I pulled myself back to his brainstorm.

"It's a generous gesture," I paused.

"Why do I feel like there's a 'but' coming next?"

"I assumed we'd rent or sell it, bring in a little money," I said, squirming inside as I heard how the words sounded. "I thought you were going to have a garage sale and get rid of a few things. Then we would decide about the trailer."

"There's no need for a garage sale," he said. "Let's move everything down the road. Your house is plenty big for all this." He swept his arm around, sloshing coffee onto the gold linoleum.

Holly Beth, my four-month-old puppy, scampered over to it.

"Holly, stop that," I snapped, grabbing a paper towel with one hand and scooping her up with the other. "You're way too young for caffeine."

She licked my face and burrowed under my chin, and Chris laughed. I wasn't quite sure what to do with the dog, our first wedding gift, a surprise from Mayor Eva Hillburn.

Chris leaned in to kiss me, but Holly Beth moved between us, nuzzling his cheek.

He stroked her soft white fur, still focused on his grand plan. "I can get a couple of buddies to haul my stuff a few days ahead of time. That way Maria and the boys can be in here before our wedding. Mama will be thrilled if I stay with her and Daddy for a while."

"It's all happening so fast," I said. "I see now why they recommend a year to plan a wedding."

Chris placed Holly gently on the floor with her favorite toy, a squeaky rubber newspaper, and pulled me over to the tweed plaid couch, similar to one my friend Marti had when we met twenty years ago.

"You're not getting cold feet, are you?" he asked, wrapping his arms around me. "I'll get rid of my junk. I love you much more than my wagon-wheel coffee table."

"I didn't realize all the decisions we would have to make. Maybe we should have eloped."

"No way. I intend for all of Green to be there when Pastor Jean pronounces us husband and wife. It'll be a day to remember."

"No doubt the locals will talk about it for years." I cuddled next to him, his arm draped around my shoulders. "They'll tell how that hussy from Ohio stormed in here and took the town's best catch."

"Are you snuggling or stalling?" Chris asked after a couple of moments.

"Both. Let's talk about the house later. I need to check on Iris Jo. Will you take care of the little princess while I'm gone?"

"Of course I will." He picked the puppy up as he helped me into my jacket, lifting my dark ponytail over the collar and kissing my neck, while Holly licked Chris's face and yelped as though she had never been happier.

"I was afraid that was going to happen," I said, opening the door. "She likes you better than me."

He made a big smooching sound, pretending to kiss the puppy and then giving me a little peck on the cheek. "Surely you're not jealous of your own dog."

"Don't be silly."

His three dogs jumped around us when we stepped outside, and I reached into my jacket pocket for treats. "But I'm not above bribing your dogs to love me more."

Walking the short distance down the gravel road, my steps slowed as I worried about Iris,

14

undergoing chemotherapy for breast cancer. A key newspaper employee and confidante, she lived between me and Chris, our places spread out on Route Two. Tiny Grace Community Chapel sat across the road.

The winter air was chilly but the signs of early spring were evident: a flock of robins migrating through, the tiniest of green leaves on trees, and jonquils budding in the shallow ditch. Spring was about to burst forth, and everything would be new and fresh for our wedding day, a symbol of my new life in Green and the roots I had put into the red Louisiana clay.

When Chris had proposed on Christmas Eve, we wanted a short engagement, egged on by family and friends who had tried to push us together for more than a year.

"Don't you think you've dragged your heels long enough?" asked newspaper clerk and photographer Tammy. "You're not exactly a spring chicken."

"Speaking of spring," Iris Jo, peacemaker of the group, said, "how about March or April? You love North Louisiana in springtime."

"Don't plan it too close to the Easter cold snap," Katy, a high school intern, said. "Spring dresses look silly under coats."

"Katy's got a good point," Tammy added. "The weather's pretty unpredictable that time of year."

"When's the weather not weird around here?" I asked.

Before the New Year rolled around, my mind had turned to planning a spring wedding, a beautiful late March day, the perfect time to become Lois Barker Craig, an honor I did not take lightly. I could see flowering quince in big urns at the front of the church, mixed with mock orange and early dogwoods, and maybe a redbud branch or two. I would carry lilies, and ask Miss Barbara, a cranky advertiser who owned a clothing store, to find me a dress.

A journalist for more than two decades and owner of *The Green News-Item* for more than two years, I thought the deadline of a wedding would be easy.

Had I only known.

My mental to-do list added item after item. I woke up in the middle of the night and jotted notes on a tablet I kept by my bed, and taped notes on doors at home and work. With less than a month to go, I needed to finalize my family's travel plans, empty a closet for Chris, and plan coverage to fill the upcoming editions of the newspaper, not completely trusting anyone else. Tammy called me bossy, but I preferred to think of it as leadership.

Now I had another issue to consider. I had spent months looking for ways for our community to serve people in poverty. *Was I too stingy to offer shelter to a precious family?*

The mobile home was not much by the standards of many of the people I had worked with in Dayton, nor in the eyes of those who lived in fancy houses on Bayou Lake in Green. When I first met Chris, widowed five years earlier, I wondered why a man who taught school and had land with ponds would not choose a better house.

"I like it out here," he told me when we started our evening walks, the strolls that turned into romance. "The bright stars. The open space. I'm not a fancy guy and I don't need a fancy house." We had never spoken of it again.

As I drew near to Iris Jo's house, Stan, all-around production guy at the paper and recent boyfriend to Iris, backed out in his giant blue pickup, his window whirring down when he saw me.

"I brought a little breakfast, but she's puny," he said. "Thanks for coming. You always make her feel better."

I waved and walked around the house, tapping on the door to the den, a room made from an enclosed carport. "It's me," I yelled, going in without waiting for a reply.

Iris, only slightly older than me but wiser and, well, more mature, was propped up in the overstuffed recliner she had bought before her surgery. She gave a small smile when I entered.

"I'm here to hold your hair back as needed and

ask for marriage advice," I said, leaning over to give her a careful hug.

"I'm past the throwing-up stage today and don't have enough hair to hold back, so I'll pass," she said. "But I'm happy for your company."

I sprawled on the couch, at home in her small ranch-style house. I tried not to wince when her cat, Earl Grey, appeared from the kitchen, climbed up on the back of the sofa, and swiped at my hair. What was it with me and animals?

"Early, baby, leave Lois alone," Iris Jo said. "You know she's not your biggest fan."

"He's OK," I said, scooting over slightly. "As long as you don't give me a kitten for a wedding gift."

"Holly Beth still wreaking havoc?"

"I never knew how much work puppies were," I said. "She's not an A student at housebreaking, and you've seen what happens when I take her to the office. Tammy and Katy spoil her rotten, and she cries at night to get out of her crate. Don't tell Chris, but she sounds so sad that I've let her up on the bed."

"Have you taken Mayor Eva off the guest list for springing a dog on you?"

"It's hard to hold it against Eva when Holly's so sweet. She's more lovable than her mother." Sugar Marie, the mayor's Yorkie mix and Holly Beth's mother, had bitten me on the face last year and had a bit of an attitude problem, if you asked me.

"You mentioned marriage advice," Iris said. "Since you've only been engaged three months, isn't it a tad early for trouble?"

"My loving husband-to-be thinks we should give his trailer away. I'm not so sure."

"Does he have a recipient in mind?"

"Maria, from the Spanish service at church, and her sons."

"That sounds like something Chris would do."

"So you like the idea?"

"He's not going to be my husband," Iris said. "Your opinion is the one that matters."

"Chris says if they lived closer, the church could help more. Doesn't that seem a little over the top?"

"What's over the top?" Tammy waltzed through the door right as I spoke. Iris and I waved and said hello, and Earl Grey jumped down to rub against Tammy's leg. She picked him up and tickled him on the throat, the cat purring as loud as the hum of an old refrigerator.

"Traitor," I muttered.

"Lois is not trying to outdo me and Walt with a big wedding maneuver, is she, Iris?" Tammy said, sitting next to me with the cat on her lap. "I had the Florida-beach-wedding idea first, and we're going on a cruise for our honeymoon. Late summer. Mark your calendars."

Tammy had grown up in Green, worked at the front counter and took pictures for the *Item*, and was used to being in the middle of everything. If she wasn't the center of the action by happenstance, she put herself there.

"What's over the top?" she repeated, looking from me to Iris. Today, the budding photo-journalist seemed closer to Katy's teens than her own late twenties, sitting on the couch in tight jeans and a long-sleeved chiffon shirt.

"Chris wants to give his trailer away," I said.

"Wow," Tammy said, her eyes widening. "I hope Walt doesn't do that with his house because I'm not sure where we'd live. My apartment's tiny."

Tammy's future move pained me, so I ignored the comment. Her fiancé was an attorney in Shreveport, about an hour away, and I thought it unlikely she would commute.

"It's possible I'm not all that excited about my groom's giveaway idea," I said. "I should be . . . I have a great house for Chris and me."

"A house that Aunt Helen *gave* you," Tammy said. "You can help someone the way she helped you." Twirling a big bracelet on her arm, she played with the cat, unaware that she also played with my emotions. My beloved house on Route Two had been a gift from Helen McCuller, deceased friend, mentor, and former owner of the newspaper. It anchored me in the little community. Chris and I could do the same for Maria and her children.

"How dumb can I be?" I asked.

Iris and Tammy looked at each other and smiled. "That's a rhetorical question."

"You're the smartest person I know," Tammy said.

"I'm a hypocrite. I've preached to everyone for months to help newcomers, and I'm miffed that Chris wants to do just that."

"Welcome to engaged life," Tammy said. "You aren't used to Chris making decisions that affect you. That's hard, especially for a woman like you."

"A woman like me?"

"You want to call the shots," she said.

I looked at Iris, quiet, with a gentle manner. I could tell she was trying not to laugh.

"I do, don't I?" I asked.

"Lois, you help everyone you cross paths with," Iris said. "But most of us like being in control. That's what I hate most about this cancer. It wasn't in my plans."

"Marrying Walt wasn't in my plans either," Tammy said. "Talk about bowling me over. We never know what's around the corner."

"Somehow all the twists and turns work out," Iris Jo said. "You and Chris will make the right decision."

"He already has," I said. "I've got to go."

I headed for the door and turned back to give Iris a kiss on the cheek.

"I'm going to tell him his idea is brilliant. Then I'm going to suggest he donate his decorator items to charity."

• • •

Chris and I met the next afternoon with Maria and Pastor Jean in the parsonage next to Grace Community Chapel. Jean, dressed in the skirt and blouse she had preached in, settled the trio of boys in front of a cartoon DVD and came back into the kitchen where we sat.

"*¿Hay algo mal?*" Maria asked Jean, looking tired and a little worn.

"No, no," Jean said and patted her hand.

Once more frustrated by my lack of Spanish skills, I glanced at Jean and Chris, both of whom were learning the language at a quick pace. My studies were interrupted by impatience and a decided lack of devotion to vocabulary words.

"Maria wants to know if something is wrong," the pastor said. "She's had so much bad news these past few months. I told her this was a good thing." She smiled at the younger woman and touched her hand softly.

Maria, one of Green's many Mexican immigrants, had lost her husband in a logging accident in a nearby parish. She regularly attended the Spanish-language service Pastor Jean had started, a controversial ministry among church members who didn't want "those foreign people moving in."

"Lois and I have a gift for you," Chris said.

"A gift?" Maria asked, and then smiled, her

white teeth beautiful against her dark skin. "More clothes for my boys?"

"*Una casa para sus hijos*," my fiancé said in his new Spanish. "A house for your boys."

"We want you to have it," I said.

"For me?" Maria asked.

"For you," Chris and I said at the same moment.

I turned to Jean, inspired by her relentless efforts to meet both the spiritual and physical needs of her flock. "Let's have a party and give items for the house. No hand-me-downs."

"A new kind of bridal shower. I like the way you think, Lois. I'll start spreading the word while you show Maria the place."

Maria seemed almost dazed as we escorted her across the road and into the trailer, the boys more interested in the dogs than the tour.

"How much?" she asked after we looked at bedrooms and pointed out closets and cabinets.

Chris and I looked at each other, puzzled.

"How much the rent? I don't think I can afford."

I engulfed her in one of Green's well-known hugs, tears flowing down my cheeks and Chris's eyes glistening.

How much?

How much courage it took for her to build a better life for her children. How much energy to make decisions every day without understanding the language.

How much?

"*Gratis*," I said in one of the few Spanish words I had mastered. "Free. Our wedding gift to you."

Looking at the trailer through Maria's eyes reminded me how much a home of your own mattered.

How incredible it would be when Chris moved into our home on Route Two, the simple old house that would be filled with love.

2

You missed a treat if you weren't at Mary McHeart's pooch party for her eight-year-old poodle, Prissy, last Friday. A three-foot-tall cake was made in the shape of a doghouse, and the pile of presents was described as "bigger than Mt. Everest." Nearly twenty dogs were on hand to celebrate, and, needless to say, it was a lively event. The only problem occurred when basset hound Daphne got a little too frisky with Elvis, a visiting schnauzer. This reporter's Rascal was a perfect gentleman.
—The Green News-Item

When I opened my eyes, I knew the perfect headline for the hours ahead: "Historic Day! Lois Barker Getting Married!"

Most headlines don't get exclamation points,

but this story ranked right up there with the biggies. For years I wondered if I would ever find a husband. I was as lousy at waiting as my puppy was at using the bathroom in the right place.

When I found Chris, I realized what I had been waiting for.

To think that he had been down in Green, Louisiana, waiting for me to come along at just the right moment. Early this evening, a gorgeous spring Saturday, we would wed before family and friends at Grace Chapel, the tiny church where my awkward approach to faith was being molded into something better. What an incredible moment it would be!

We would start married life in a hotel near the airport in Shreveport and leave the next day for a week at a cabin in Montana, a secluded hideaway with no phones or news stories or friendly meddling.

Thrilled, I hopped up, surprising Holly Beth, settled on the pillow next to mine. She barked and began to chase her tail, her excitement mirroring what I felt. "Come on, silly girl," I said, scooping her up and laughing. "We've got a big day ahead of us."

I turned the coffeepot on and stepped out the side door, setting her in the yard. She explored, and I drank in the perfect spring morning. Tender new leaves glowed with the early light, and a streak of orange sparkled in the sky. This was the kind of day I had hoped for when we chose our wedding date.

The forsythia was brilliant yellow, and tiny wood violets nestled in the low spot next to the driveway. The green spikes of a clump of Louisiana irises had shot up next to the slab of the garage, which was burned by one of the paper's former owners in a series of fires intended to run me out of town. Thank goodness those days of intimidation were over. Chuck McCuller was dead. His brother, Dub, was on probation, and that horrid politician and crooked realtor, Major Wilson, was behind bars.

Chris and I looked forward to a nice, calm life as a married couple, the newspaper hassles of the past two years behind us. One of our first projects was going to be to rebuild the garage, with a workshop attached to the back.

When the phone rang, I grabbed Holly, steadied my coffee, and began what had become a familiar dash. The old house relied upon Aunt Helen's rotary phone, and I spent a lot of time running for it. Perhaps Chris and I should invest in a cordless, although I liked to look out the kitchen window while I talked, standing at the sink, or sitting at the little pine table, my feet propped on a chair.

I picked up the black receiver. "Wedding Central," I said. I expected the phone to ring off the hook all day.

"Is it bad luck for the groom to talk to the bride before the wedding?" Chris asked.

"Most definitely not. Good morning, husband-to-be. We're getting married tonight!"

"Thank goodness. I couldn't stand this madhouse much longer. You shook things up in Green when you took over the paper and moved down the road from me, but that was nothing compared to this wedding."

"I'll rescue you in twelve hours," I said. "Are things crazy at your parents' house?"

"That's putting it mildly. Daddy says the shirt he's supposed to wear is too tight around the neck, and Mama told him he would go without a tie over her dead body."

"Like father, like son."

"To top it off, Mannix won't stop barking. Maybe we should have left all the dogs on your porch till after the wedding."

"Are you kidding?" I asked. "I wish I had sent Holly Beth over there. She wiggled all night."

"That wouldn't be a problem if you didn't let her sleep with you," Chris said. "Maybe Daddy can break her of that while we're on our trip."

"We'll see. They'll get her right after the service, right?"

"We'll be fortunate if Daddy stays through the reception. They have the world's largest box of dog bones and a rope toy for her."

My future mother-in-law's voice could be heard

in the background, and she sounded agitated. One of Miss Estelle's worst habits was carrying on a conversation with you while you were on the phone with someone else. According to Chris and his brothers, she had done it for years.

"Wait a sec, Lois. Mama's saying something."

I stretched the phone cord over to the far counter and poured breakfast for Holly, freshened her water, and patted her gently. I was going to miss the silly little thing.

"Mama's updating me on the weather. She's been glued to the television since the rehearsal dinner last night. Did your brother have to mention the possibility of rain?"

"We're a pushy sort of family, in case you haven't noticed. He wanted to make sure everyone brought umbrellas."

"Pushy or not, it's great they're here for the wedding," my groom said. "I'm glad they approve of me, because there's no way I'm not marrying you."

"After all these years of me being single, my brothers probably would have approved of that donkey down the road."

"Oh, that's a real compliment." He laughed.

"They had begun to tell their kids to take care of me in my old age."

"I'll take care of you, baby. I keep reminding myself that no matter how crazy today gets, tomorrow morning we'll be on our way to Montana."

"Husband and wife," I said. "Alone at last."

"I'd better go talk Mama down off the ledge. She's worried about a thunderstorm warning." His voice got softer. "I can't wait to see you tonight."

"I'll be the one in the long white dress."

The phone rang again before I got out for a morning walk, a sentimental stroll I planned to take on Route Two.

"Is this Lois Barker, bride-to-be?" My best friend Marti's voice came in loud and clear, despite being halfway across the world.

"Marti, I'm getting married! It's happening!"

"Oh, Lois, I should be there with you, wearing an ugly dress and throwing rice in your hair." She sounded as though she were about to cry.

"You're right where you are supposed to be. Remember our deal? You and Gary will visit in the summer, when it's hot and humid and we're all settled. You can see my new collection of catfish memorabilia."

My best friend, newly married to a seminary student in Dayton, had booked tickets for a spring mission trip to the Congo shortly before my engagement. Marti had been devastated when I told her the wedding date, trying to bail out of the trip or to convince me to reschedule.

"Is it nice there today?" she asked.

"It's dazzling. A classic spring day."

"Have a wonderful time tonight," she said, "and

29

don't fret about anything. It's your day, dear friend. Love you."

"Love you, too. I'll e-mail Tammy's photos in a week or so. She's gotten so good that you're not going to believe your eyes."

My brother had been right, darn it. It was going to rain, but maybe it would hold off until after the ceremony. Clouds had gathered in the west, but it was a spring day to savor. A steady breeze blew, and the air cooled off by the hour.

I strolled through my house and around my yard for the last time as a single woman, holding Holly close. I picked the first bloom off the unusual pink dogwood tree in the front yard and put it in my journal, stacking two books on top of it. It'd be a sweet reminder when we got back. I loaded my honeymoon suitcase into my little car and grabbed the box with my new shoes.

I stroked Holly and put her in her crate with her favorite blanket. "Mr. Hugh will be here to get you in a little while," I said. "You be a sweet girl while I'm gone."

I didn't even like animals. Or so I thought. I could barely stand to leave her, even though I knew she'd get as much attention as a child at my in-laws' house.

In-laws? How strange that sounded.

My heart sped up as I pulled into the Grace Community parking lot, between the church and

Pastor Jean's house, nervous all of a sudden, and then laughed at the church sign, which usually had a catchy slogan that Jean found online. Today it said, "CONGRATS, Lois & Chris!"

Kevin and Jean waited by the side door of the church, big smiles on their faces when I drove up. Kevin, my best friend in Green, hummed "Here Comes the Bride."

"You barely missed your reception volunteers," Jean said. "They've got everything set up and have run home to get dressed."

The wind gusted when I opened my car door, and it nearly snatched my suitcase from Jean's hands. "Don't chip those nails," Kevin said when I closed the trunk. "Watch your hair. I don't want it all tangled when I put it up."

"Where did that wind come from?" I asked. "It was beautiful an hour ago."

"An ordinary spring storm," Jean said. "Happens every year in Louisiana."

"Spring storm? Those clouds look like something out of a horror movie."

"You'll think 'fairy tale' when you see the church," Kevin said. "Let's get inside before the rain starts."

I started toward the side door, but they steered me to the front. "Close your eyes." Jean grabbed my arm.

I walked cautiously up the steps and into the minuscule foyer.

"Look what your friends have been up to this afternoon," Jean said. Kevin pulled me further into the church.

A profusion of spring flowers in pinks and whites greeted me. Each window had a small glass vase with ivy from the woods nearby and small bouquets of tulips and bridal wreath. Antique candelabras stood on each side at the front, ivory tapers waiting to be lit. A banner hung to the side with dogwood blossoms appliquéd on it. "And the two shall become one," it read.

"Who?" I asked, too overcome to say more.

"The church women mostly brought flowers from their yards," Kevin said. "Becca from the flower shop made sure it was natural, just like you wanted."

"Iris and her small group made the quilt," Jean said. The previous banner had been hung after the death of Iris Jo's teenage son, Matt, in a car accident. "Iris said it was time to change."

"Now it's time to change *you* before everyone gets here," Kevin said. "We've got to get that hair done, and Barbara brought your dress by earlier. It's more beautiful than I remembered. I didn't know she designed it herself."

My cranky advertiser had been insulted when I asked to order a dress at her shop. "Order, my hind leg," she snorted. "I'm going to sew you a dress."

With visions of double-knit and support

stockings, I gave my best newspaper-owner resistance, to no avail. "Give me one shot at it," she said. "I've been sewing party dresses for years, so I don't see why I can't make a wedding gown."

I gulped and said OK.

The dress was stunning.

Using Jean's office as the bridal parlor, Kevin carefully brushed my hair, pulling a small section back with wispy dark curls around my face and spraying it extra stiff. "We can't have it blowing out of place when you leave the church," she said. Then she added blush, which I tried to wipe off. "You're keyed up," Kevin said. "Stand still. You don't want to look pale."

Kevin and Jean—friends, supporters, physician, pastor—slipped the wedding gown over my hair. The elegant fabric slid coolly down my body, the strapless bodice covered in lace, the skirt flowing slightly. Jean carefully placed the veil in my hair, and I tearfully asked Kevin to fasten my mother's pearls around my neck.

Katy and Molly burst in, both wearing pale pink dresses in different styles, eager to assume their places as ushers and to voice their opinions on every topic that came up.

"Wow," Katy said. "You're going to blow Chris away. That dress looks like one you'd order from New York, not downtown Green."

A piercing whistle signaled the arrival of my

33

wedding photographer. Tammy snapped pictures as she walked in, pausing to whistle again. "Fabuloso dress. You clean up real good."

She glanced down at my feet. "Have your new shoes been chewed on?"

"Take one guess," I said. "I hoped no one would notice."

She held up her frayed camera strap. "Holly Beth got this last week and my wallet the week before."

"She may be the cutest wedding gift ever, but she's certainly not the easiest," Kevin said. "I'm glad Asa Corinthian hasn't taken up that habit. Pray for Papa Levi tonight. He's watching Asa, and, as you know, my son can be a handful."

"Are you sure he can't come to the wedding?" I asked. "You know Chris and I don't care if he makes noise."

"Lois, my idea of a beautiful wedding does not include Asa racing the bride down the aisle. Besides, I have a date with Terrence."

Tammy squealed. "That hunk of a lawyer from Alexandria? The guy who helped Lois with the lawsuit against the paper last year?"

"One and the same."

"I didn't know you two were dating," Katy jumped in.

"This is our second date. I hope a wedding doesn't scare him away."

"Did you know?" Katy turned to Molly, always

wanting to make sure she was not scooped on a piece of gossip.

"I'm Dr. Kevin's backup babysitter," Molly said. "I know all."

"You sneak! Best friends are supposed to tell each other everything."

"Forget about telling everything," Tammy said. "I need to get photos of everything, including the guests arriving. I hope everyone doesn't get soaked before I get good shots."

"Soaked?" I asked. "Is it supposed to rain that hard?"

"When I checked a few minutes ago, it looked like the front's going north of us," she said, "but it could be bad later on."

"Who's posting the online news update?" I turned for Kevin to straighten my hem, my head twisted toward Tammy.

"Tom's got it covered," Molly said. "He's not over that stomach bug, so he'd planned to skip the wedding anyway. He didn't think you—or Dr. Kevin—would appreciate him infecting the town."

"He's got that right," Kevin said.

"I think he's secretly afraid he'll cry," Molly said. "He's a lot more tenderhearted than he lets on."

"Maybe that's why he never got married. He couldn't stand going to weddings," Katy added.

"He wants to stay near the police radio," Tammy said. "Lois, he said to tell you he'll hold down the fort."

3

Bouef Parish beauty Misty Bright was crowned queen of the Red Clover Festival Saturday, outshining a field of ten contestants parading atop a flatbed trailer. The day got even better for the 19-year-old dental assistant when, her tiara perched on her blonde hair, she won her division in the festival's annual arm-wrestling competition. Her 16-year-old adversary, Heather Hull, put up a good fight and had praise for Misty. "Losing to a girl with a crown was the most depressing thing. But there's no denying she's fast and real strong for someone with such skinny arms."
—The Green News-Item

On the arm of my oldest brother, I stepped into the sanctuary and instantly met Chris's eyes. He inhaled deeply, put a hand over his heart, and smiled.

The lights were turned low, and candles flickered. The flowers looked and smelled as though we had wandered into a beautiful garden, as I had dreamed. Guests stood in unison as the pianist pounded out the "Wedding March." My dress flowed, and my heart soared.

I stopped to hug my soon-to-be mother-in-law,

handed my bouquet of stunning lilies to my young niece, and moved on to the altar, where I placed my hand on top of Chris's. Pastor Jean stood nearby, Bible open.

The sound of sniffles could be heard over a strong wind outside. Katy stood and read a Scripture passage, and Jean spoke quiet words about love. Chris and I didn't take our eyes off each other throughout the vows.

"For longer than I care to admit, I have looked forward to uttering these words," Jean said with a smile, rain pounding on the roof. "Chris and Lois, I now pronounce you husband and wife."

My heart skipped a beat.

"Chris, might I suggest you kiss your bride?" Lightning shot through the stained glass windows, and a huge clap of thunder boomed when Chris put his lips to mine. The lights in the church flickered. The crowd applauded, and Tammy set her camera aside long enough to let loose with another of her celebrated shrill whistles.

"Each of you," Jean said to the guests, "has helped Lois and Chris make it to the altar. We all know that was not the easiest thing to do." Cheers, groans, and more clapping burst out.

"Lois doesn't do things the easy way," Rose, the owner of the antique mall across from the paper, yelled.

"You can say that again," the usually sedate mayor said.

"Amen," said Kevin.

Chris had his arm around my waist and gave me a tight squeeze. The grin on my face felt as though it reached both ears.

"Each of you, friends and family, are part of their marriage. They will need you to laugh with them and share their tears through the years." As the pastor spoke, I wiped one of those tears from my eyes with an antique handkerchief Rose had given me for the occasion.

"Please rise and join hands, making a covenant to love and encourage them as they love and encourage you."

Chris and I, hands linked, faced the congregation, as the people who meant so much to us gathered nearer. My new mother-in-law took my right hand, tears in her eyes, and Jean took my husband's left hand, herself less composed than usual.

There were a few moments of shuffling and movement and chatty conversation, punctuated by what had become a fierce storm outside. Tammy scooted around the room, looking as though she had photographed weddings for years, instead of this being the first time.

Marcus took the hand of Pearl, his bride of many years, and of Kevin, the daughter he was so proud of. Kevin clasped attorney Terrence's hand, and Terrence wound up holding hands with Walt, a funny sight, with Linda, reporter Alex, and the mayor next to them. Molly and Katy had their arms around each other, best friends forever, and Iris and Stan were also linked, arms around their waists.

A group of newspaper correspondents, including Anna Grace, the food writer, and Bud, the agriculture guy, clustered together; and Hank, the fire chief, and Doug, the police chief, who had helped us through the terrible year of the fires, stood on the edge, clearly trying to avoid holding hands with each other but whispering after a particularly loud peal of thunder.

I closed my eyes briefly, trying to capture the image forever in my mind, faces illuminated by candlelight and the persistent lightning outside the stained glass.

Chris held up my left hand with my new wedding ring, never letting go.

"Isn't this something?" he said to the guests, and teary smiles met his as the lights flickered again. Another murmur flowed through the crowd, and I was unclear whether they were talking about our wedding or the storm.

"Pastor Jean will lead us in prayer before we take you folks to the fellowship hall for cake and punch," Chris said.

"Merciful, loving God, thank you for Lois and Chris. Give them an abundance of love for each other and those they encounter wherever life leads them." A huge clap of thunder sounded, lightning glared through the window, and the church almost shook with the wind. "And guide them through the storms of life."

Our guests gave a nervous laugh, and the wind blew so hard that the small church swayed. Or maybe it was my weak knees, overcome with happiness.

"Friends and family, I present to you Green's newlyweds, Lois and Chris Craig," Pastor Jean said. The crowd clapped, and my husband held me tight against his solid chest.

Right before the lights went out.

My to-do lists had let me down. Not one of them included flashlights for the reception.

Thankfully, Hank, used to guiding people at fires, safely herded everyone into the fellowship hall. Stan and Walt helped Chris move candelabras from the sanctuary. I noticed Doug conferring with Chris before he went back into the main church building.

"What am I going to do about the pictures of you and Chris together?" Tammy wailed, sounding a great deal like the wind through the side door. "I need portraits. And I can't photograph the reception in the dark."

"Tammy, we'll do the best we can," I said.

"The lights go out all the time on Route Two," Iris Jo added, "and it usually doesn't last long."

With candles and three flashlights dug out of a

box in the storeroom, we came up with enough light to serve the beautiful two-layered square wedding cake with pink polka dots on white icing, and the groom's cake, shaped like a giant catfish with licorice whiskers.

Chris and I stood to the side as people congratulated us, hugging me and high-fiving my groom, a level of anxiety apparent as the crowd tried to figure out whether to stay put or try to make it home in the rain.

The journalist in me noticed the instant Hank and Doug left the room, and I nudged Chris. "Maybe you should talk to the chiefs. See what's up. I'll visit and distract everyone."

I motioned to Tammy. "See if you can reach Tom and find out what's going on. Use the phone in Pastor Jean's office. The cell reception is horrible out here."

By now the storm was so loud that my niece and nephews were clutching their mothers' legs, and Katy and Molly had a rare worried look on their faces. Hank and Doug reappeared and motioned to the mayor, right as Chris headed my way and Tammy burst back in. In a rare show of restraint, she pulled us into the small kitchen, where a church member was trying to mix more punch by flashlight.

"Tornado warning," Tammy said, quiet and to the point. "Tom says it's bad to the west of us. Two twisters have been reported on the ground in

East Texas. Everyone needs to take cover immediately."

The police and fire chiefs and mayor walked in, and the volunteer making punch laid the flashlight down and scurried out. "It looks bad and could be headed our way," Doug said. "Tornado paths are hard to predict, but we need to prepare for the worst."

"Do what you need to do," Chris said.

Doug stood on a chair, his flashlight steady. "Friends, do not panic," he said, words I always thought were designed to make people freak out. "Take cover now. We have reports of a possible tornado in the area."

His words catapulted the room into motion. The flimsy plastic chairs fell to the floor as people stood quickly. A few people said, "Lord, have mercy," while others pushed to get into place.

"This side of the room, walk quickly to the kitchen," Hank said in a loud voice, motioning with a flashlight. "This side, follow Pastor Jean to the largest of the Sunday school classrooms."

"No shoving," Doug said. "Stay away from windows."

Chris reached for me, and I looked around the room for his parents, who did not move as quickly as the younger people. Estelle and Hugh were walking into the kitchen, chatting with a neighbor like they were at a church social.

"Lois?" Kevin's urgent voice was next to me in

the darkened room. "How bad is it? I tried to check on Papa Levi and Asa and couldn't get through."

"Tom told Tammy about ten minutes ago that it doesn't seem as bad in town as it is out here."

"I've got to go to Asa," Kevin said. "He'll be scared. Will you keep an eye on Mama and Daddy for me?" Terrence stood behind her, a hand on her back.

"No one should leave right now," Mayor Eva said. "I know you're worried, but we need everyone to take shelter." She spoke in a voice as calm as if preparing for the ice cream festival and as firm as though dressing down the city council.

Before Kevin could reply, the rain hit heavier on the roof. "Hail," Chris said.

"Get down as low as you can," Doug yelled. "Cover your heads."

Then came the roar.

Chris tackled me to the floor, and Terrence shielded Kevin, who was moaning Asa's name over and over, intermingled with "my baby, my baby."

"Our Father who art in heaven," I could hear Marcus saying from the kitchen, and those around him joined in the Lord's Prayer.

At that moment the roof peeled off a corner of the room, blowing candles over and starting three or four small fires, rain gushing in to extinguish them. Wedding debris flew around the

43

room, pieces of it sucked up through the ever-widening hole in the roof, as though a giant vacuum cleaner were at work. Buckets of rain poured into the church, and the sound of glass breaking was mixed with unknown thuds from outside.

Screams could be heard from the other areas of the church, along with loud wailing prayers for God to have mercy.

"Stay down, wherever you are," Hank yelled, barely audible over the storm. "Nobody move."

"I love you," I said to Chris, whose body protected mine. "I don't want to die."

"I love you, too," he said. "Don't let go of me."

The fury seemed as though it would never end. Seconds seemed to last for hours.

At about the time I thought my heart might stop, the winds calmed and the rain slowed—and panic exploded, people shouting for their loved ones, some separated in the mad dash for safety.

"Tammy," I heard Walt yell.

"Stan, where are you?" Fear sounded in Iris Jo's voice.

"Do *not* move," Hank shouted. "This is a dangerous situation."

"No kidding," Katy said from the kitchen. After her smart remark, I could hear her talking quietly. "We're all fine in here, Chief," she said, "but Miss Pearl has hurt her arm."

"Mama?" Kevin rushed toward the kitchen. I

slowly stood up, my knee throbbing where it had knocked into the floor.

"Chris, keep things together in here," Hank said. "I'll check with the mayor and Doug in the other rooms."

People began to scurry, but didn't seem to know where they were going. Many ran for the doors, desperate to check on family members not at the wedding.

"Do not move," Hank bellowed, already hoarse. "We are in a state of emergency."

"Get Dr. Kevin," the police chief yelled before Hank got out of the room. "Possible heart attack."

Kevin paused, torn between her mother and another patient. Her mother, huddled near the kitchen door, immediately spoke. "See to the others, baby," Pearl said. "I'm OK."

I had never felt so helpless in my life.

"What do we do?" I asked Chris, noticing blood on a cut on his hand.

"We have to figure out how bad it is outside." He spoke quickly. "We've got to make sure it's safe before we let people head out. It's going to be hard to keep them here."

"Outside?"

"On Route Two. Downtown. We dodged a bullet, but who knows what the rest of Green is like?"

"This was dodging a bullet?" I spoke slowly, rattled to the core.

"No one was killed here," Chris said. "The damage is bad but the building didn't fall in on us."

Suddenly it hit me what Chris was saying. The path of a tornado I had covered outside Dayton appeared in my mind.

"Oh, no," I said. "The *Item*. Tom. Maria and the boys. Holly Beth. I've got to check on them."

"Lois," Chris said, "one thing at a time. Let's take care of everyone here, and then do what is needed next."

Hank and Doug calmly directed everyone into the sanctuary, which seemed to have the least damage, although it was hard to tell in the darkness.

"I know you want to check on your houses and loved ones," Eva said from the pulpit. "But as your mayor, I ask you to stay until we assess the extent of the damage. It is not safe to leave."

"Maybe it's limited to this area," Bud, a volunteer patrol officer as well as part-time news correspondent, said. "Tornadoes have strange patterns."

"We can only hope that is the case," Eva said, futilely hitting redial on her phone as she spoke. "We must make sure all citizens of Green are accounted for. The police chief and I are headed into town to take control of the command station where we have a generator. Regular phones are

46

out, and cell circuits are overloaded. When we establish that it is safe, we'll get you all home."

Jean stood by Eva and suggested everyone pray. "Bow your heads alone or in small groups, as we wait, and ask for strength and wisdom and for help for those who need a special touch at this moment." She moved from person to person, laying both her hands on their shoulders and praying with them.

I walked out of the sanctuary, torn between checking on my house and Holly Beth and assisting others. My brothers followed me, asking how they could help.

"Come with me," Chris said. "We need to know what we're dealing with."

As they started to walk out the door, I ran to Chris. "Wait," I said. "I'm going, too."

"Pull things together inside," Chris said. "Start a list. We're going to need your organizational skills." He gave me a quick hug and walked out into the dark night. I could only see the branches of an unfamiliar tree near the steps.

Molly ran up to me, tears in her eyes. "Miss Lois, I've got to get home. My brothers and sisters were alone while my mother was at work. The oldest is only twelve. I've got to get to them."

"Not yet," I said. "Be patient."

"Anna Grace is almost certainly having a heart attack," Kevin said, striding in from the other

47

room. "We must get her to the hospital. Her pulse is erratic, and she's not in good shape. I think Mama's wrist is broken. Other injuries?"

"Minor," the fire chief said. "I'll drive you and Anna Grace, and you can monitor her. Bring Miss Pearl."

"I'll take your father home to check on Asa and Levi," Terrence said. Kevin's lovely face was tormented, and I knew she wanted to make sure her son was all right.

"Kiss him for me," she said. "Let me know as soon as you know, even if you have to come to the hospital."

"I'll take good care of him," Terrence said.

"Take Molly with you, Terrence, and help her out," I said. "She needs to find her mom. Be careful."

"Mayor, I'll meet you and Doug at the emergency center at the courthouse," Hank said. "Stan, you and Chris take over out here for the time being. Make sure all residents are accounted for."

"Do visual assessments as you travel," Eva said, turning into an emergency leader before my very eyes. "Watch for fallen trees and power lines and do your best to get messages to the courthouse. Don't take unnecessary risks. We need everyone safe."

Chris and my brothers walked in at that moment, their faces grim.

"It's bad, Mayor," Chris said in the most somber voice I'd ever heard. "The road is covered with uprooted trees; utility poles have snapped. It's still raining. I hope we got the worst of it out here."

Tammy grabbed the skirt of my stained wedding gown and pulled me to the side. "What do you want us to do?"

I looked up to see my newspaper staff flanking me, looking like castaways from a TV reality show, their nice clothes on, dirty and torn.

"We've got to get coverage of this online," I said. "People need to know what's going on. We'll need lots of photos, but those will be tough since it's so dark."

"Everyone will be worried sick about their relatives in Green," Linda said. "How can we get word out that people are safe? We need an online site of some sort."

"What about building damage?" Katy asked. "We need a list of that, too."

"An inventory," Alex said. "Emergency contact numbers. Shelter information, insurance adjusters. But we don't have landlines, cell service, or electricity."

"The first thing is to find out how severe the storm was and post a notice online," I said. "Alex, that's your job. Get to the courthouse, and post it quick, but don't take any more chances than you have to."

"I'll drive Tammy around town to get pictures," Walt said quietly. "If necessary, we can go to my office in Shreveport to post them."

"Thanks, Walt. Linda, take a statement from Eva, Hank, and Doug before they get out of here," I said. "Don't be pushy, but tell them we're trying to help."

"Katy, get quotes from people who were here. Tammy, let's hope you have shots of those they interview. We'll match them up later."

"If there's no Internet downtown," Tammy said, "call Walt and dictate the info. I'll go by Tom's and see what he knows. Even if he doesn't feel good, he'll pull through for us."

"Cells will be iffy," I said, "but post as you can. Remember, lives are at stake, so make sure you're accurate. But be fast."

Suddenly, I wanted to pull them back to me.

"This is important work," I said, "but it's not worth risking your lives."

"You either," Iris Jo said.

"I'll head to the newspaper," I said. "Everyone except Iris meet me there as soon as you have information. Communication will be key."

"Except me? What does that mean?"

Stan walked up and put his arm around her. "Iris, you don't want to overdo it. You can check in tomorrow. Don't forget, you had chemo this week."

"I hardly think I'd forget that," she said.

50

"Check on your house," I said, "then decide what to do."

"We'll get through this, Lois," Iris Jo said.

"I know," I said, although I wasn't that certain.

"I'm sorry about your wedding," Katy said. Tears rolled down her cheeks, and she brushed them back as though embarrassed.

The others nodded. Iris, Linda, and Tammy hugged me. Alex touched my arm.

My staff raced off in every direction. My husband was nowhere in sight. I supposed the honeymoon was off.

4

Florence and Elmo Barnhill invite everyone to a come-and-go elk chili supper at their house. "We'll be using the fish cooker, since our power's still off. We don't want to waste all that good meat in the freezer," Miss Flo said. "If you've got something you want to add to the pot, bring it along."
—The Green News-Item

Flashlight in one hand and my arm in his other, Chris guided me down the steps of Grace Chapel, not exactly the exit I had planned.

The tornado had come with a sharp drop in temperature, and the beautiful spring day seemed like it belonged to someone else. Chris put his suit coat around my shoulders, and we set out for a quick check of our house before heading our separate ways. On our wedding night.

"We should check on Maria and the boys first," I said. "If they were in that trailer, they must have been terrified. We'll have to make it fast, though. There's so much to do."

The mobile home where Chris had lived until a week ago looked unharmed, except for a tree down on the chain link fence. A faint light glowed through the window.

We walked across the road, past the church sign, turned on its side, with letters blown off. It now read, "RATS, Lois and Chris." A hysterical laugh caught in my throat, and I pushed it down. Chris knocked on the door, and I called out. Maria appeared, the children quiet in the background. A tiny battery-powered light, a gift at the house-warming party we had thrown for the family, sat on the carpet nearby.

"Are you all OK?" Chris asked.

"*Si*," she said. "It was very loud. But we have light, and we make up stories. Thanks to you, we were safe."

"Thanks to us? We put you in a trailer in the path of a tornado." I said. She didn't understand, the same way I didn't understand how the day had turned out.

"This house very strong. Not like our old house," she said. "I'm sad about your wedding.

You look beautiful." I had forgotten I was in my wedding dress.

"Thank you, Maria. Be safe."

"I'll take care of that fence when things settle down," Chris said.

"If that trailer didn't blow away, everything else must be okay," I said to Chris as we walked on down the road. "Maybe the church was the only casualty. Like Bud said, tornadoes are weird. Thank goodness those children did not lose their new home."

"Or their lives."

Fallen trees partially blocked the road, and we sloshed in and out of the muddy ditch by the road, the water halfway up to my knees.

"We'll get Holly Beth, make sure everything's safe, and go from there," Chris said. "I know you want to get to the paper as soon as possible. I need to get Mom and Dad home, make sure your family's back at the hotel."

Everything was eerily dark with the power out and not a star in the sky.

"Who knows?" Chris asked, false cheer in his voice. "We might even make our flight to Montana tomorrow."

"I wish we had bought the trip insurance."

Stan's pickup was in Iris Jo's driveway, and the couple stood staring at the house, split in two by an enormous tree, my friend's head nestled in the curve of Stan's arm.

"How bad is it?" I asked, cutting through the yard.

"The big oak took out half of the house," she said, "but Stan says he'll help me rebuild."

I rushed to comfort her. "I know the house meant a lot to you. You and Matt had special memories here."

"It's only a house. It could have been so much worse. We weren't hurt or killed. I'm sorry your wedding day turned out like this. Whose idea was it to have a spring wedding anyway?"

"If you hadn't suggested it, I probably would have come up with it on my own. You know I wanted to beat Tammy down the aisle."

"Well, you're married, and it was a beautiful service."

"The reception left something to be desired," I said. "I knew I should have gotten the fondue pots." The small talk seemed to make things more normal, as though we weren't standing outside her broken home in wedding clothes, a ball of fear in our guts about the rest of Green.

"Are you headed to the paper?" Iris asked.

"After we pick up Holly Beth." I peered down the dark road. "Chris says we probably have roof damage, since the church got hit so hard, but he's got a tarp. Do you want to stay with us?"

"Heavens, no." She laughed. "You're newlyweds. I'm staying at the Lakeside Motel until I figure out what to do. Pearl and Marcus said they have plenty of room."

"Lois," Chris called, "why don't you let Stan and me take a look at our place? You stay here with Iris."

"No way. I've got to check on Holly Beth. She's probably peed all over her crate by now."

"I doubt that I'll make it to the paper tonight," Iris said. "But I'll send Stan as soon as he drops me off. He can get the generator going if the power's off downtown."

"I'll be there in thirty minutes, and everyone has assignments. Hopefully it won't be too bad."

Chris and I walked on, adrenaline fueling our pace as we rounded the small corner and looked over at our house.

It was gone!

My eyes simply could not believe what I saw— or rather what I did not see.

Chris didn't say a word, just stood with his head cocked at an angle as though the house might magically appear. A moment of pure insanity washed over me.

"Where is it?" I asked.

"Lois . . ." Chris said in a voice meant to comfort me, a husband's voice.

A treasured giant pecan tree was uprooted, and trash was spread everywhere in tiny bits and pieces.

Nothing was recognizable, not sofa or table or

refrigerator or . . . Holly Beth. I started screaming her name, running into my yard, afraid of what I would see.

Chris caught up with me in an instant and put both arms around me, pulling me close. "Sweetheart, catch your breath. We'll find her. Everything's going to be okay." He sounded as though he doubted the words himself.

"We have to find her," I said, sobbing. "She was trapped in her crate. It's so cold and so dark and—" I was being ridiculous. The chilly night was the least of Holly Beth's problems. Had the house smashed her? Had she been blown away and killed by the impact?

My mind raced as my legs tried to do likewise. I lifted the skirt of my dress and tore around where the house had sat, no crate in sight. *Nothing here,* I thought, and had a crazed mental picture of Chris's giant catfish pillow flying through the air.

Was this what shock felt like?

"I've never seen anything like it," Chris said, refusing to leave my side when I suggested we split up to search. "It's completely gone." I could almost see him shifting mental gears. "The stuff has to be somewhere."

"Unless it was blown to bits."

Together we walked the boundaries of the yard, calling to the puppy. "I didn't even want a dog anyway, and now she's lost. And you gave your house away, and we don't have a place to live."

I knew the fear and anger in my voice were unfair. But this was not the way I had intended to spend my wedding night.

Instead of lashing back at me, as I would have done to him, Chris grabbed my hand and pulled it to his cheek. "Let's keep looking."

Suddenly he started running. "Lois, there." He pointed up, and I thought perhaps he had lost his mind.

Holly Beth's crate sat in the top of an old crape myrtle.

"Shhh," Chris said. "Don't say anything. If she's alive, we don't want her to jump around and fall. I'll get the ladder." As quickly as the words left his mouth, he seemed to realize there was no ladder.

"I used to be quite good at this when I was a boy," he whispered. My husband of less than two hours climbed the gnarly tree as though he did it every day. I heard him murmuring as he lifted the crate.

"She's alive," he yelled. "I can't tell if she's hurt, but she's glad to see me."

As he slid down, I stood at the trunk of the tree and took the heavy crate from him, my shoulders groaning with the strain. I set it on the ground, opened the gate and gently spoke to Holly. "Are you okay, baby girl?"

She leapt out of the cage and jumped around me, running over to Chris. She looked as though nothing had ever happened, licking both of us and barking what I thought of as her happy bark.

"Oh, Chris, she's all right," I squeezed my dog close. "She's OK."

"I would not have believed it if I hadn't seen it with my own eyes."

Holly Beth ran over to where the house had stood and looked back at us, barking louder now. Then she raced around the edges of where it had been, as though surveying the land.

"It's truly gone, isn't it?" I asked.

"Lois, I'm so sorry. I know how much this house meant to you."

"It's only a house."

Chris insisted on taking me to the paper after we made a quick stop at Grace. No one, not even Pastor Jean, was around, my car the only one in the parking lot. Even in the dark, it was obvious the church listed to the side and the parsonage looked weather-beaten.

I got my suitcase out of my car and shoved it next to Chris's, behind the front seat of his truck.

"At least I have clothes to wear," I said.

As we drove into town, the capriciousness of the storm stunned us. Cars were thrown everywhere like toys. A four-wheeler was perched on a wooden fence. Several buildings in a row would be demolished, while the house next door would look unscathed. Utility poles were thrown everywhere, and the occasional electrical transformer sizzled and sparked.

"Look, over there," I would say, and Chris would follow with, "Can you believe that?" and point to more devastation. Cotton trailers were turned over and strewn across a field, barely visible by headlights. A little tin utility shed sat in the middle of the road, and a tractor was upside down in a ditch.

"Surely it can't be this bad all over town," I said and punched the numbers on my phone for what seemed like the thousandth time with the same result. "All circuits are busy."

Chris drove slowly, dodging limbs and an assortment of unidentifiable debris. My worry grew with each sign of damage.

"I'm worried sick about little Asa and Molly's family. What if your parents' house is torn up? And we need to check on your dogs," I said.

Chris laid his hand on my knee. "One thing at a time. We have to have faith that everything is going to be OK."

"Faith?" My nerves erupted. "I gained a husband today but lost a house. Anna Grace may be dead, and we don't know if the paper is standing. I had planned to be on my way to a honey-moon suite, but I'm going to try to cover a big story with the journalistic equivalent of a kindergarten class. My faith is in short supply at the moment."

"We'll deal with this together," he said. "No matter what else happened today, we got married."

"I knew it was going to be one for the history books," I said, "but this took it a little too far."

"Lois, are you prepared for what you may find at the *Item*?"

"No" I said, hugging Holly Beth. "I'm not sure of anything. I have to cover this story. I don't even know where to begin."

"You'll figure it out," he said and then hesitated, an odd husky sound in his voice. "The paper and the church seem indestructible."

"They are more than buildings," I said, pulling myself together. "They don't need a building to make them real." My words worked up a new layer of energy within me, what I suspected Chris was trying to do.

"I'm going to have lots of busy days ahead of me," I said, attempting again to get my cell phone to work. By the time we reached downtown, the police and sheriff's departments had barricaded off most of the streets, standing guard against potential looters and unknown hazards. The flashing blue lights illuminated damage a moment at a time.

The young deputy who had so annoyed me during many of the fires stood near the turn we would have to make to get to the building.

"Sorry," he said, leaning in as Chris rolled his

truck window down. "Can't let civilians downtown tonight. Not safe."

"Son," Chris said, "if you think you're going to keep my wife from her newspaper, you obviously don't know who you're dealing with."

"Oh, I know Miss Barker, all right," he said.

"That's Mrs. Craig to you," Chris said. While they spoke, I slipped out of the truck with Holly Beth.

As I started running, both the deputy and Chris called after me. I stopped and turned.

"Are you wearing a wedding dress?" the deputy asked.

"Unfortunately, I am."

"Go on through," he said, moving the barricade so Chris could drive past. I hopped back in the truck and we drove down Main Street. Most of the buildings, including Mayor Eva's department store and Rose and Linda's antique mall, looked fine, but in the dark it was hard to tell.

As we turned into the parking lot of the *News-Item*, I covered my eyes with my hands.

"I can't look," I said. "You tell me."

"She seems to be all in one piece."

We walked through the littered parking lot, and with shaking hands, I unlocked the front door. Chris, Holly Beth, and I stepped into the newspaper.

"Tom? Tammy?" I called, but no one answered.

"Now what do I do?" I said to Chris. "For all the

61

big stories I've ever covered, I've never been in a situation like this."

"Why don't you change clothes while I try to get the generator running? By then you'll have a plan of action."

In the dark of my office, I slipped the beautiful gown off and rubbed the fabric against my face. When I let it drop to the floor, Holly Beth grabbed it with her teeth and began to flop it back and forth. I couldn't help but laugh, and then hot tears filled my throat.

Slipping into jeans and a long-sleeve T-shirt, meant for a hike out West, I heard a faint whirring sound, and the lamp in the lobby came on. My wonderful husband had gotten the generator going. It seemed like a big victory in that moment.

Chris inspected the building while I got the computers booted up, with no Internet service. I typed in a list of stories and tried to think of how we would handle the twice-weekly print version, due out on Tuesday.

Pacing around the room while I worked, Chris furrowed his brow and kept trying to place a call on his cell and the newspaper phones, to no avail.

"You have to go," I said. "You're on the emergency team and you've got to check on your folks and my brothers, clear roads, or help with who knows what."

"I won't leave you here alone," he said.

"I can't go anywhere," I said. "Tom will be here any minute, and Alex, too. You're needed on Route Two."

"I won't leave you here alone," he said again.

"You're my husband, not my bodyguard," I said, trying to use a smile to soften the words. "You know you've got to get out there."

"I'm concerned," he said. "But I won't leave my bride until someone else shows up."

The sight of Alex coming through the front door had never been so welcome.

My only true reporter, a veteran at age twenty-three, had discarded his tie, but he wore loafers rather than his ragged tennis shoes and looked more mature than usual in his wedding slacks and nice shirt, dirty though they were.

"How bad is the damage?" I asked.

"Beyond bad," he said. "The mayor wants you at the command center. Chris, she needs you to meet a crew at the Grace Chapel parking lot."

"Fatalities?" I asked.

"Yes."

"How many? Who?" Chris asked.

"I think that's what the mayor wants to talk with Lois about. She won't tell me."

"Chris, I've got to go," I said, grabbing my purse, an extra notebook and a small digital camera. "Alex, you stay here and keep your fingers crossed that we get phone service back. Help Stan and Tom work up a plan for an extra edition for tomorrow afternoon. I'll be back as soon as I can."

"Take a laptop, boss," Alex said, handing me one of the two portable computers the newspaper owned.

Chris looked agitated. "I'm going to the motel to pick up your brothers and head out to see what needs doing. I'll plan to meet you back here in four hours. If you need me before then, send Alex or Stan. I'll use Mama and Daddy's place as a base."

"If it's still there," I said.

"It will be," he said. "It has to be."

I rushed into Chris's arms and held tight. "I don't want you to go."

"I'll be back," he said, pulling my head to his shoulder. "Be careful, Mrs. Craig."

"I will," I said, unable to come up with a clever response. "I love you."

"I love you, too." He kissed me gently on the mouth. "You were a beautiful bride."

The front door swung shut, my husband out in the pitch black night, the beam of his flashlight already gone.

"Lois, are you OK?" Alex asked.

"Not yet," I said, shaking my head. "But we know how to cover the news, and that's what we have to do. Lives depend on us. Have you heard from any of the others? Tammy or Katy? Linda? Anyone?"

"Everyone's spread out, but we agreed to check in here. I haven't run into Tom, but he posted a story at seven-thirty saying a massive storm was headed our way. I did two updates from the courthouse. We scooped everyone, and the Associated Press has picked up my first story."

"The wire services are following this?"

"I'd say everyone in the country is following this."

5

*A loose billy goat has been impounded
by Bouef Parish officials after chasing
calves on local farms. A deputy found the
goat and is attempting to identify the owner
because "this seems to be a real good quality
animal." If the owner is not found, the
goat will be adopted or sold at auction.
If the sheriff's department has got
your goat, give them a call.*
—*The Green News-Item*

Eva Hillburn, flanked by three or four men, including the police and fire chiefs, pointed to a large map of Bouef Parish. Her back was to the door of the basement command center, and the room around her buzzed like the yellow jacket nest Chris had stirred up while mowing my yard last summer.

I stood silently at the back of the room, taking in as much information as I could without getting in the way.

"We have to go here next," Eva said, pointing to the core of town with her coral manicured fingernail. She wore the silk suit she had on at our wedding. "Door-to-door, block-to-block until everyone is accounted for. I feel certain that damage is extensive in this neighborhood. The houses were practically falling down as it was."

Jerry Turner, the banker who had run against Eva for mayor, sat hunched over a map on a tan metal desk and slammed his hand down on a nearby metal desk. "No," he said. "We know outlying areas are hard hit. We can't waste time on inner-city neighborhoods that may be fine."

He looked at Hank and Doug. "Don't you agree, boys? We start in the area and work our way back. We don't have enough manpower to cover the entire town, so we'll have to count on citizens to work out problems we can't reach."

"Jerry," Eva said in what I thought of as her stately mayoral voice, "this is no time to argue."

"I know what we need to do," the banker said. "Serve the people we know are hurt. Look for others next. There's plenty of work to go around."

Eva took a deep breath. "We're wasting valuable time," she said. "You handle the parish. I'll take the city limits. We'll divide volunteers into teams with captains to report back on the hour, every hour."

"That'll work," Hank said.

"Good idea, Mayor," Doug said.

She turned and surveyed the room, catching sight of me. "I'll be right with you," she said, all business. She turned back to the officials nearby. "Hank, we need an emergency medical technician with each group if possible. Doug, assign the groups and get them on their way. Volunteers are meeting upstairs."

"Lois," she said, turning to me, "we have a crisis beyond what we're prepared for. We've notified the National Guard and declared a state of emergency. We've confirmed two deaths, and that's likely only the beginning. Injuries are piling up faster than the hospital can handle them. It's operating on a generator and has serious roof damage."

At the word "deaths," my mind froze. "Anna Grace?" I whispered, knowing she had been in bad shape when she left the church.

"Last I heard she was stable," Eva said, "but things are so chaotic that I don't know for sure."

I could tell there was something she was holding back.

"Who, Mayor?" I asked. "Who are the fatalities so far?"

"There's no good way to tell you," she said. "Your copy editor Tom and Papa Levi . . ."

"Tom? Are you sure?"

"A tree crushed his car. The vehicle was found blown off a side road out toward Route Two," she said quietly. "A neighbor flagged down a deputy, but Tom couldn't be saved. He was dead by the time help arrived."

"He was trying to warn us," I said. "He knew we were out of touch during the ceremony, that no one would have a phone on."

"Tom's last actions say a lot about the kind of man he was," Eva said. "He tried to send a text telling everyone to take cover, said it would be horrific."

"If he only had come to the wedding as planned."

"Lois, this is not your fault. There is nothing you could have done."

"Asa?" My voice shook.

"He's fine, other than a bruise or two. He was crying in the bathtub, surrounded by pillows, when Terrence and the others got to him. Levi was under a mattress in the hall. Apparently he had been trying to drag it to the bathroom. Most of the windows were blown out."

I put my head in my hands, and the mayor laid manicured fingers on my arm.

"Sugar Marie?" I asked, going through my mental list.

"At Dub's house. He kept her during the wedding." Dub McCuller was one of two brothers

68

I had dealt with in the purchase of the newspaper and not one of my favorite people.

"How's Holly Beth?" Eva asked.

"We found her in her crate in a tree. She seems fine."

"A tree? Did you leave her on the porch?"

"She was in the kitchen. Aunt Helen's house is gone."

"Gone?"

"No longer there. It disappeared," I said, and I could see her processing that image. "Your house?"

"A few shingles off and my beautiful camellia uprooted, but nothing more, according to Dub. My side of the street looks like nothing happened, and the houses across the street are a mess."

"I never thought about how random a storm could be. To think that this day started so beautifully, barely a cloud in the sky."

"We've conducted a very preliminary check," Eva said, pushing her hands through her hair in a gesture I'd not seen before. "Thirty to thirty-five percent of the buildings appear to be destroyed. Many more are damaged. We have long days ahead of us."

Green had unquestionably elected the right mayor to deal with a tragedy. I tried to imagine former Mayor Oscar Myers, elderly and set in his ways, handling this.

"The wedding ceremony was lovely," Eva said,

pulling a tissue from her pocket. She wiped her eyes and straightened her hair. "I have to get back to work. Your staff can use that desk in the back there."

Tom was dead.

Big, sloppy, wordaholic Tom, who loved crossword puzzles and books and edited copy as though he worked on the biggest newspaper in the country, who coached Katy so she could become a true reporter, who led our editorial crusades and cared as passionately about *The Green News-Item* as he had when he walked in the door forty-one years ago.

"This newspaper is here to stay," he'd proclaimed in a loud voice a few months ago. "No Internet or cable television will kill it. Only lazy journalists will be able to do that."

Likely the paper had killed him, coming to spread the news to his coworkers, even though he was not feeling well and didn't like to drive at night. My heart ached at the thought of telling Katy and the others, but I didn't want them to hear it from anyone else.

I glanced at the big clock on the wall over the map, frozen at seven forty-eight when the power went off. I looked down at my watch and held it up to my ear.

"It hasn't stopped," Hank said, walking up with a clipboard. "It really is only nine twenty-five."

"It feels like a time warp," I said.

His walkie-talkie squawked, and he stepped away, listening, his expression more stern by the moment. "I have to get back out there, Lois."

"Can I get quotes and an update from you first?"

He nodded and sighed deeply. "Two more confirmed dead."

"God help us," I said, half in anger, half in prayer.

"I don't have names on the others. I'll keep you posted."

"If you see Chris, will you tell him I'm OK?"

"Sure thing," he said. "Congratulations, again."

I tried my cell phone again. Nothing. *Would it be better to stay at the command center or go back to the paper?*

The mayor had mentioned satellite service, so this could be a good place to set up shop and stay up on breaking news developments. The metal desk in the corner would be a serviceable news center for a while, but how could we coordinate coverage without better phone service? I longed for electricity and our little newsroom, Tom at the center, laying out pages, conversation whirling around me as we struggled to find enough news to fill the paper.

Even in this room surrounded by people I knew, I felt lost and alone.

For the next ten minutes, I resorted to doing

what I do best—gathering information and piecing together a short article. Law enforcement personnel came and went, including volunteers who regularly helped on fire calls and with routine police matters. With each new person, a look of dread mixed with the need to know washed over faces, sick-looking under the fluorescent light of the basement room. The headquarters already smelled stale and felt stuffy.

Bud, the agriculture columnist, came in wearing his polyester Green Auxiliary Police uniform, what Katy liked to call his GAP outfit. Before I could reach him, a half dozen people mobbed him for news from the world outside.

He stopped speaking when he noticed me. His back was stiff, and I thought he was too old to be out this late, helping with such a tragedy.

"Tom handled my copy every week for more than thirty years," he said. "We've lost a good man."

I pulled out my notebook and pen. "Will you give your thoughts for the paper?" I asked, trying to hold back tears. "I want to post his obituary as soon as possible."

"First, I need to update the mayor with word from the police chief," he said. I followed as he walked over to Eva and pointed to the map. She picked up several small pins with blue heads and began to push them into neighborhoods.

I now understood what the words *deathly quiet*

meant. Everyone in the room paused to watch. As Bud referred to notes, Eva pushed another pin into the map, then another.

"Friends," Eva said, while Bud folded up the paper and stuck it in his pocket, "confirmed deaths are now at five. We are awaiting word from out in the parish."

I sat down at the desk, turned on my laptop, and began to write, relieved to see a weak Internet connection.

Alex and Tammy came in after I hit send on the latest online update.

"Is it true about Tom?" Tammy asked. "Did he really die?"

"Yes," I said. "It's true." My voice trembled, and Tammy and I moved toward each other.

"It's hard to imagine putting out the *Item* without Tom," Alex said.

"I leaned on him to choose photos," Tammy said. "I've got a few good shots now, but if he were here, he'd tell me to get better ones when the sun comes up."

"I can't let myself think about it yet," I said. "Let's focus on putting out the best paper we can. I want us to put out an extra edition, one that would make Tom proud."

"What happens now?" Tammy asked.

"Stay here and get what you can, Alex. Update online every fifteen minutes and gather details for the special edition. I'll go over to the paper and send someone to relieve you when I can. Tammy, find us the picture that will tell the story in one glance."

Alex was already on his way to the coffeepot before we got out of the room, and I noticed he had changed into the ratty tennis shoes. The moment of familiarity felt good.

Stan and I were about halfway through mapping out a four-page extra for the next day in the newsroom when Iris Jo strolled in wearing a warm-up suit and baseball cap, a familiar brown accordion file in her hands and a tote bag on her shoulder.

"Are you OK?" Stan asked, rushing over to her.

"If you think I'm going to bed while everyone else works on the biggest story we've ever had, you're wrong," she said. "Knowing Lois, we'll have an extra edition by this time tomorrow. We have to figure out where we'll print it and how we'll get it there."

"Tell me you didn't drive out to your house to get those files," Stan said.

"Picked up comfortable clothes, too. I couldn't think straight when I first saw the house, but I'm better now."

Iris Jo was a poor cousin of the McCuller family, which had owned the paper for decades before I bought it. From the first day she unlocked the door and let me in, I knew Iris Jo had held the newspaper together for years. My profit-sharing plan for employees cased my guilt that I wound up with the *Item* instead of her, but she insisted she wanted to work at the paper, not run it.

She dug in the tote bag. "Where's Tom?" she asked. "I made sandwiches."

Stan and I locked eyes. I knew he would speak the words.

"Darling, it's not good news," he said softly, putting his arms around her. He wore his usual pressroom jumpsuit but looked like a different person as he soothed Iris. "He died in the storm."

"Tom, dead? But he's always worked here," she said, almost visibly shrinking as she took in Stan's words. "This place was like home to him. He'd come in on weekends and take a nap on that dirty old couch right there."

I knew it was my turn to talk when Katy, Molly, and Linda trooped into the newsroom thirty minutes later, but the expressions on their faces told me they had heard the news.

"Tell us it isn't true," Katy said, walking over to Tom's desk and staring at the array of oddities he kept there. Her eyes were red and swollen. "Please tell us it's a bad rumor, that the cops got it wrong, that it was someone else."

"I wish I could."

Before I could move, Katy, tears rolling down

her cheeks, picked up the old-fashioned green visor that Tom put on the minute he walked into the newsroom and took off the minute he left.

"How will I know how to write without him to help me?" she asked.

"He was so nice to us, said we weren't half bad for kids," Molly said, so somber she looked as though she might break at any moment.

"The death count is up to six," Katy said softly. "I suppose you know Asa's grandfather was among them."

I nodded. "Molly, is your family all right?"

"They went over to the nursing home where Mama works," she said. "That place has a generator and is taking in old people. I promised her I'd be careful and probably wouldn't see her until late tomorrow."

"I dropped my parents there, too," Linda said. Her parents both suffered from dementia, her mother's severe. Their care, along with her accounting work at the paper and her co-ownership of the antique mall across the street, kept her busy, but she was determined to become a top-notch reporter.

"The school was hardly hurt," Katy said. "They're opening a shelter for people who don't have a place to stay. That's one of the oldest buildings in town. I don't understand." I hated the bewildered look on her face, but it matched the way my brain felt.

"Alex said you want to put out an extra edition tomorrow," Linda said.

"I do." The words sounded odd for a moment. Had I uttered them in front of the church this very day?

"I don't even know what an extra is," Katy said.

"It's a special edition of a newspaper when there's a big story," Molly said. "I didn't think anyone did them anymore."

"They're rarely produced," I said. "But this is a historic day in Green. We'll offer it as a service to our readers, single copy only. We won't try to deliver it to houses."

"Good thing because there aren't that many houses left," Linda said.

Everyone gravitated to Tom's desk, despite my thought that we would move to the conference room. Tammy and Walt arrived after we started.

"Deaths?" I asked as soon as they walked in the door.

"Seven," Tammy said, moving to the group, tears running down her face. "Two dozen critically injured at the hospital here, with a dozen more transported either to Shreveport or Alexandria. Many less serious but needing medical care. Here are pictures." She turned her digital camera to me, and I squinted to see.

"You need glasses," she said.

"I'll run right out and get a pair."

She put her arm around my shoulder, gave me a

slight squeeze, and then stepped back to photograph the staff at work on the paper.

Within minutes we knew we needed consistent electricity and Internet access to prepare the pages in the morning. They could be e-mailed to a press yet to be arranged.

"Bossy is out," Stan said, referring to our old press. "She won't run off this generator."

I gathered my thoughts while Linda and Katy wrote preliminary stories, and Tammy worked on her photos. Walt sat in the corner, conferring quietly with Iris.

I made two trips to the courthouse to check in with Alex and hear what Eva had to say. Walt, whom I had dated briefly when I moved to Green, walked with me both times "for protection," leaving Tammy to edit her photos.

As we walked out of the newspaper building, I stumbled on the stairs, and he took my arm.

"I didn't intend to spend my wedding night with you," I said, trying to make a joke but on the verge of tears.

"I'm sorry about Tom and Levi . . . and your wedding day," he said, "but I'm thankful you're in Green. I don't know of anyone else who could have handled this story the way you will."

"Thank you," I said and straightened my shoulders. "I hope you're right."

A new group of volunteers had arrived at the command center, and Eva ruled. Her voice was scratchy, but she looked as professional as if it were a weekday morning at the department store she owned.

"You need rest," I told her. "By light of day we both know the work will be greater." I glanced over at the contentious Jerry, snoring with his head on a desk. "We'll need you to lead us."

"The roads are almost impassable until we get trees cut," Eva said. "I'm planning to sleep upstairs in one of the nice quiet courtrooms. We may not have power back for a few days, but they're trying to get special equipment downtown. Phones, too. They said it could be a week or more. The governor's office called. He'll be here within a day or two."

Walt and I walked silently back to the paper.

With emotions as scattered as my possessions, I called Linda and Molly to my office. "I need you to go to the hotel room Chris and I have reserved in Shreveport. It's the only way I can think of to make sure we get the paper out with no power here. Linda, you have the best computer skills. Molly, you're going to need to lay out news pages since Tom isn't here. Can you do that?"

"I can try," Molly said.

"Set up the computers, get a few hours of sleep, and have the pages done by eleven tomorrow morning. I'll e-mail headlines and photos and check the pages from the computer in the courthouse.

"Tammy, go to Walt's and post pictures and expanded updates. You'll have to type these stories in," I said, pulling the pages out of the printer. "Include a request for reader contributions—eyewitness stories, photos, whatever they've got. The only way we'll be able to do this story is with help from the community.

"We'll have a lot of ground to cover at daybreak," I said. "Stan, will you make sure Katy gets home safe and get Iris back to the Lakeside?"

I glanced down at my updated to-do list. "Iris, ask them to hold a room for Chris and me if they possibly can. Tell them we may need it for quite a while."

Blank stares greeted me. In the drama I had forgotten to tell them about my house.

"It blew away," I said. "Let's call it a day."

"Before we go," Katy said, "we have one more thing to do."

She dug around in her desk and came up with the paint used to list the names of those who died on the front window, a long-standing *News-Item* tradition, to keep readers informed between editions.

We walked together to the lobby and stood silently while she painted the words. "Tom McNutt. Awesome Journalist. Our friend."

Everyone had left by the time Chris returned to the paper, carrying two sleeping bags borrowed from his brother. As soon as I unlocked the front door, he laid the gear down and folded me into his arms. He looked as tired as I felt.

"Your family?" I asked. "The dogs?"

"Every house is damaged one way or the other. That big pine in the side yard at Mama and Daddy's is now in the guest bedroom. My brothers will take care of them for the time being, but I need to tell you something else."

A dozen names ran through my mind before Chris could continue. "Who?" I whispered.

"Mannix. He's hurt, and I'm not sure he'll make it. When the tree fell, he was trapped under the metal roof on the back porch. The vet doesn't have power and he's helping injured people as well as animals. I always thought it was a cliché, but it's a war zone out there."

I had a soft spot in my heart for Mannix, the big mutt who had terrified me when he wound up on my porch injured. He reminded me of how tentative and fearful I had been when I first moved to Green.

"We can't lose Mannix," I said. "We can't."

"We've done all we can," Chris said "Let's set up camp in your office and try to get a little rest. Tomorrow will be a long day."

The warmth and strength of my husband comforted me as I fell asleep. Holly Beth snuggled beside me.

Could the best day of your life also be the worst?

6

The Dramatic Director of Greater Green Theatrical Society, who lives in the Cold Water community, has issued an emergency change-of-plans announcement for the group's summer production.
"While we had our hearts set on The Wizard of Oz, *we have decided to perform* I Told You So, *a play written by Green's own Patricia Pullig. Tryouts will be announced after things calm down."*
—The Green News-Item

A commotion outside woke me.

"We've got company," Chris yelled from the lobby.

"Don't they know it's rude to pop in on newlyweds?" I mumbled, running my hand through my tangled hair and frowning down at the wrinkled clothes I had slept in. For a split second the memory of the tornado eluded me, skirting around my brain like a wasp looking for someone to sting.

"You're probably going to want to see this," my husband said, louder this time.

"Behold the bride," I said, walking into the lobby, trying to smooth my hair and my shirt at the same time.

"Good morning, wife," Chris said. Wearing a pair of warm-up pants and a Green High Rabbits shirt, he looked like an advertisement for an outdoor catalog while I felt like a candidate for a TV program on how not to dress.

A gargantuan motor home was parked in the newspaper lot, and a crew of people in matching T-shirts scurried around, setting up a satellite dish and a host of items I didn't recognize. The sun was barely up, but the artificial lights made it look like midday.

An attractive, familiar-looking woman was applying lipstick, no mirror apparently needed, and even at this distance I could see her rub her tongue over her teeth and practice a smile.

"What in the world?" I asked. "Who are those people, and why are they in my parking lot?"

"You're the journalist here, but I'm guessing that would be the media," Chris said.

I turned the bolt and stepped outside, distracted at once by the tornado damage visible by daylight.

"Look at my beautiful Bradford pears," I said to Chris. "They're split in half." Bloom-filled limbs lay on the pavement. "Wonder where the awning from the antique mall went?"

Chris pointed to the paper rack lying on its side in the parking lot, Rose's awning perfectly balanced on top of it. An ice chest lay next to it.

"Were you witnesses to the tornado?" a voice

asked from a few feet away. "Did you take shelter in this building?"

I turned to see a young African American man with a clipboard standing near the bottom of the steps. He had the name "Byron" stitched on his shirt, right over a network logo.

"May we help you?" Chris asked.

"We'd like to interview you for a broadcast on the Green tornado," the man said. "We'll be live in five minutes."

I glanced at my watch. It was six fifty-eight, nearly twelve hours to the minute since the sanctuary doors had opened and I had started down the aisle toward Chris. The beauty of the moment flickered across my brain.

"I'm Lois Barker—ummm, Craig—Lois Barker Craig," I said, holding out my hand. "I'm the owner of the local newspaper. You're going to need to move your vehicle because my staff is due any minute."

My voice sounded rude, but I longed for even a snippet of control. Besides, our extra edition wouldn't be out for at least five hours, and I didn't like seeing the competition in my own front yard.

"You'll have to take that up with my boss," the news guy said. "We drove overnight from Atlanta and we're about to start our broadcast. I'm Byron, breaking news producer."

"I believe I'll leave this one to my wife," Chris said. "Lois, I'm going to do a quick check around the area. I'll meet you back here in fifteen minutes."

"Coward," I said into his ear as he reached in to give me a hug.

Rose walked over from her antique shop, around the corner of the gigantic van. "Well, if it isn't the newlyweds," she said. "Don't you think the RV is a bit much?"

I could tell she was trying to be cheerful, but she looked worn out and her eyes were swollen.

"The media," I said in an exaggerated snarl. "Can't take 'em anywhere."

"Oh my," she said and held up a grocery sack. "I didn't bring enough biscuits for everyone."

"Biscuits?" Chris said, turning quickly.

"Did you get power back?" I asked. I wasn't sure which of the two thoughts excited me more, food or electricity.

"Gas stove," she said. "I came to check on things at the antique mall. Figured you and Chris wouldn't be sharing a romantic breakfast, so brought a few things. I'm here to help in any way needed."

"Do you have a tow truck?" I asked.

"Ma'am, I need you immediately," Byron said, tapping his foot and eyeing the biscuit Chris was wolfing down.

"I'll be right back," I said.

"Your name again, ma'am?"

"Lois Barker Craig," I said. "Owner of *The*

Green News-Item. I realize this is an unusual circumstance, but you can't block our building."

As I walked with him to the van, one part of my mind surveyed damage and cataloged the extensive chores ahead of me. The other wanted to push the TV crew out of the way and regain control of my little piece of Green.

"And here with me live is . . ." the attractive woman glanced down at the tablet the guy handed her, "the owner of the local newspaper, Lois Craig. Thank you for joining us on what must be a very difficult morning."

"Joining you?"

"Can you tell us about what you were doing when the tornado hit, Ms. Craig?"

"I was serving cake and punch."

"Anything else?" she asked, an edge to her voice.

"I was thinking how much fun the next few days were going to be."

I babbled my way through the ambush interview and realized I must look like one of those yokels I made fun of on national news programs.

At least I used proper grammar.

I cried when my brothers and their families came to the paper to say good-bye.

"Are you sure you'll be all right?" they asked. "We'll stay if we can help."

"Your biggest help is giving Chris and me a

room at the motel," I said, trying to keep a light tone. With people out of their homes and the influx of members of the media, spare beds were hard to come by, and I wanted to stake a claim on one for us.

"This wasn't the wedding we thought we'd be attending," one of my sisters-in-law said. "But we couldn't be happier for you. Chris is a wonderful guy."

"We like him a lot," my youngest brother said. "Never thought you'd choose such a winner."

Tears rolled freely as they climbed into their rental car. My young niece leaned out the window with the bouquet I had handed her as I walked to the altar. I touched one of the flowers tenderly. The blossoms had opened a little since last night and smelled like a new bottle of perfume.

"Do you want it back, Aunt Lois?" she asked, thrusting it toward me.

"I want you to have it," I said.

"You'd better get back to work, sister," my older brother said. "Mom would be so proud of you."

On a regular day in Green, the good-byes would have taken longer than my wedding, everyone needing to hug every member of my family and say something sweet. Today, the words were quick with a promise of a return visit.

At my insistence, Chris went to check on Mannix before he started his day of hard labor. He returned looking tireder than after an August football scrimmage game. "The vet says he's hanging on, but he didn't bounce back overnight. At best, he's probably going to lose a leg."

My head hurt as I heard the news and sent Chris off for rescue work, which was to start with a brief prayer service in the Grace Chapel parking lot.

"Give everyone my love," I said. "Tell them I'm thinking of them."

"It'll be one of the saddest church services we've ever had," Chris said.

Getting ready for the extra edition to come from a rented press in Alexandria, the staff rolled up its sleeves with grim determination, worse for wear but committed to putting together a near perfect report. The anecdotes were haunting.

"We were huddled in the hall closet when the roof blew off," a woman on a cot at the school gym said. "I thought we would be sucked right out through the ceiling."

"The hail hit my car so hard it broke the windows out," a young waitress said. "But it hardly touched my boyfriend's car in the driveway next to it."

Community correspondents e-mailed tale after tale, without being reminded.

"Miss Mattie and Miss Hattie West invite anyone needing shelter in the Pear Tree Road area to come see them," wrote one of our regulars. "We have an extra bed and plenty of rooms for pallets,"

88

Mattie said. "Hattie said to be sure to let folks know that they are equipped to handle cats."

"A photo album that appears to belong to the Dalzell family has been located in the ditch behind the home of Mary and Pete Nolen. They will hold onto it until you can get by," another correspondent wrote.

"Softball-size hail fell on the other side of Bayou Lake," one volunteer reporter wrote. "Thank goodness we don't have livestock because it could have knocked out a cow."

Nearly all of their reports included a message for me and the staff, offering thoughts and prayers about Tom and announcing their readiness to do whatever they could to help. I knew as soon as the streets were cleared and power restored, trays of homemade food would pour in.

Many stories involved hurt or missing pets, and I held Holly Beth in my lap while I edited them.

"My Colby, the bravest dog ever, shielded me with her body," one elderly woman said.

"Peanut and Pistol are the smartest cats," a farmer said. "They hid under the mower in the shed, and we had to coax them out."

"My dog shot from my arms like a rocket," a teacher from Green High said.

"My puppy flew to the top of a tree," I wanted to add.

Katy, with tears in her eyes, painted the names of the dead underneath Tom's name on the newspaper window, adding a word or two about each person.

The first extra edition of the *Item* since the bombing of Pearl Harbor was trucked back to Green by noon.

The huge headline was in all capital letters and blasted off the page: TORNADO HITS GREEN; SEVEN CONFIRMED DEAD. The smaller head underneath continued the grim news: Dozens of Buildings Destroyed; Thousands Without Power. Most of the page was filled with an early-morning photograph by Tammy of an entire block wiped clean, a tea kettle resting on a set of steps with no house in sight.

The first copies were snapped up by regional and national journalists who seemed to have been airlifted into town by the dozens. Everywhere I or any other member of the staff turned, a reporter thrust a microphone in our faces.

The mayor looked regal as she gave interview after interview. She had changed into a fresh outfit and scarcely showed any strain, even though Alex told me she stayed up most of the night and personally tried to connect with the families of those who died.

Readers lined up outside the building to get copies of the newspaper, and Stan and Iris Jo rounded up a handful of carriers to sell them by the side of the road.

Once the *Item* was produced and distributed, the

staff gathered in the conference room. Necessities were at a premium with most restaurants and stores closed, and Walt appeared with a large array of food and bottled water from a little grocery store about forty miles north. "I thought you could eat the fried chicken now, and save the fruit and chips for later."

"Some lucky woman needs to snap you right up," I said, my stomach growling at the smell of the boxes of chicken.

"Good idea, boss." Tammy gave me a friendly nudge and nestled up against her fiancé.

For a split second, things almost felt right.

Then I remembered Tom and Papa Levi and Mannix and my house and the many who were hurt and hurting. Suddenly the chicken didn't smell quite so good.

"How about if I say a blessing?" I asked. Rarely did a meal start in Green without a prayer. Never was I the one to offer thanks in a group. But if the staff was surprised, they didn't show it. I thanked God for the food and for keeping us safe and begged for strength for the days ahead.

Iris Jo, who had shown up for work before any of the others, looked at me with tears in her eyes. "Thank you for that."

The meal was to the point, like most of our conversations since the tornado hit.

"The hard part for the *Item* starts today." I wiped grease from my mouth as I spoke.

"Are you telling us last night was easy?" Linda asked. "Because if you are, I don't think I'm cut out for the newspaper business."

"The big breaking story is the easy part. Adrenaline flows, and we do what needs to be done. But this story won't be measured in hours; it will be counted in months, even years."

"We need a plan," Alex said. "I'm too old to stay up all night very often."

Tammy rolled her eyes. "Puh-lease. Since when did you get old?"

"Since the town blew away," he snapped.

Usually Tom would have jumped in here, either ramping up the argument or calming them down. I felt his loss keenly, even looked over my shoulder as though he might walk through the door.

"Will we put out a Tuesday paper as usual, or try for another one tomorrow?" Stan asked.

The thought of doing a Monday paper had not crossed my mind, and my spirits soared—then sank. The staff was exhausted after only a day, and we had spent a huge chunk of our minuscule budget on the extra. I looked around the table.

"Let's do another special edition," Katy said. "People need to know what's going on."

"I'll call our main advertisers and see if they'll sponsor it," Linda said. "It'll be a public service."

Molly had been resting her head on the table

and looked up. "I can lay it out. School's out for spring break, and I don't have many hours at the Pak-N-Go."

"We're on the priority list for power, so we may luck out," Stan said.

"We have to pace ourselves," I said, "or each of you will burn out within a week. Tammy, organize a photo plan. Linda, list the correspondents and figure out how we can utilize them. Their voices are crucial. Iris Jo can figure out how we're going to pay for all this. Alex, go home and take a nap. See you back at seven p.m. Grab news nuggets anywhere you go."

We would not be outdone by out-of-town journalists thinking they could take over our turf.

I walked over to the command center in the middle of the afternoon to establish my presence as a journalistic force to be reckoned with. The air was crisp and clear, the sun shining. It was about as different from the night before as possible.

The mayor was sitting on a bench to the side of the courthouse, a baseball cap and oversized windbreaker on. Her dressy skirt stuck out from the hem of the jacket, and she had on three-inch pink heels. If I had not found Holly Beth in a tree the night before and seen my house blown away, the sight would have stunned me.

"Running from the law?" I asked, sitting down next to her.

"From the press," she said. "I had no idea you people could be so annoying."

"Sorry. Comes with the territory."

"They're reporting the most outrageous things I've ever heard," Eva said, "and making us look like a cross between *The Beverly Hillbillies* and *Sanford and Son*."

"They won't stay long. They have short attention spans. We'll be old news in a day or two. They'll be off to cover a politician in a sex scandal or movie star sighting."

"I sure hope so. We need to feed people, find more drinking water, and get the electricity back on. I don't have time to fool with questions like, 'Mayor Hillburn, what does it feel like to see your town blown away?' What kind of idiotic question is that?"

"You've hardly taken a breath since it hit," I said. "You're handling this like you're a disaster pro, but you've lived here most of your life, have your hand in every part of Green. How *does* it feel?"

"My heart is broken, and I'm trying to hold it together for people who need me." She glanced around as though to make sure no one was looking. "I'm wearing a disguise to keep from talking to reporters, spilling my guts to my newspaper owner on a bench that wasn't here yesterday, and wishing I could go home and walk Sugar Marie."

"I can't get my mind around how we'll ever get Green back to where it was. Where are all these people going to live? Where am *I* going to live?" I asked.

"This will take every one of those leadership bones you've got in your body, Lois. Green can't do it without you and the *Item*."

"We couldn't do it without you," I said, standing. "By the way, where did this bench come from?"

"I have no idea."

7

Sondra Chaffin wants to thank all those who found homes for her daughter's pets after her daughter's tragic death. "I'm thankful to announce that Happy Girl was placed with a woman in my Sunday school class who had been praying for a new dog since the death of her June Bug in the winter." Donations to the animal shelter of your choice would be greatly appreciated.
—*The Green News-Item*

Green needed a miracle.

The late afternoon sunlight lit my office with a golden glow, and I abandoned the writing tablet on my desk and walked to the window, gazing sadly at the broken trees and noticing debris on the roof of the building next door.

It seemed as though a week had passed since my wedding, but I hadn't even made it through one full day.

"Good news. Good news. Good news. Lord, bring us some good news," I said out loud.

"Amen," a voice said behind me. I jumped and turned sheepishly to see Pastor Jean, in one of her trademark souvenir sweatshirts, this one from San Antonio.

"A miracle!" I said with a laugh, trying to act as though I had not been standing at the window talking to myself. "How'd you know I needed you right this very minute?"

"I could tell you it was a heavenly hunch," she said, "but I ran into your new husband out on Route Two. He mentioned you could use a visit."

Chris. Now there was a miracle, for sure. I reached down to touch my wedding band.

"He's on chain-saw duty with his brothers and hopes to see you in time for supper," Jean said. "They've cleared a sizable number of fallen trees, which sure makes driving a lot easier."

"If there's a silver lining to this storm, it's the right to use power tools with abandon," I said. "I've never seen a group of men more eager to get out and cut something up."

"Chris did have another message for you," Jean said with a smile. "He leaned in my car window and said, 'Tell my wife I love her.' I think he was afraid the other guys would hear him. He practically scampered back to work."

"Now that's the kind of news I like." I smiled at the idea of Chris scampering anywhere. "I hoped he'd get back here in time to drive me around town. I left my car at the church and I've been so busy with the paper that I haven't gotten out for a good look."

"I was also supposed to tell you that Chris loaned your car to Mr. Marcus," Jean said. "His truck was smashed by a tree, which also clobbered their house. He needs it to make arrangements for Levi and to help the people in his neighborhood association."

"Do you have time to take a tour?" I asked. "I need to get out of this building."

"I can check on church members while we're at it. Let's go."

"Can we drive to the hospital and see Kevin?" I asked. "And Anna Grace? Maybe by the courthouse for an update?"

"I'm at your disposal," Jean said.

I stuck my head in the newsroom where Molly sat at the computer at Tom's desk, Holly Beth chewing on her shoe while the girl concentrated on the screen. "I'm practicing headlines," she said, "and working on suggestions for tomorrow's front page. Everyone else is out."

"Don't you need to go home?" I asked.

"Linda and I are going back to Shreveport to do

the production work," she said. "It's easier that way. That hotel room was super nice, but we're going to Walt's tonight. He says we can set up a newsroom on his dining table."

"I thought we were going to use the computer over at the command center."

"All those other reporters keep shoving us away." Molly frowned. "We are now in a sort of 'pool,' whatever that means, and we have to take turns."

"A pool? How many people are over there?"

"At least fifty," she said. "There are TV crews, reporters, and photographers from New Orleans and Baton Rouge and Shreveport and Alexandria, even Dallas and Houston. You've never seen such a zoo."

"Where's Linda?"

"She went to check on her parents," Molly said. "Everything's under control."

"Right." I bent to pet Holly Beth. "Can you keep the puppy till I get back?"

"Sure, if you'll buy me a new pair of shoes." Molly smiled and scooped up my dog.

Jean and I got in her car, squeezed next to the curb. My lot was filled with an assortment of vehicles I didn't recognize. As we drove off, a handsome young reporter interviewed Katy, who gestured wildly with her hands and smiled as though she were a broadcast veteran.

"Don't they know she's only seventeen?" I

snapped. "They need her parents' permission to talk to her like that."

"And that young woman you left running the newsroom is how old?" Jean asked, shooting me her preacher look.

"OK, so I've got a double standard. You knew that when you invited me for this ride. Let's get out of here."

As we drove, I gasped and exclaimed so often that in any other situation I would have felt redundant. I had seen Tammy's photographs and the marked up maps at the courthouse, so I knew in my mind how bad the damage was. Seeing it with my own eyes overwhelmed me.

Pastor Mali from the Methodist church was unloading a van full of supplies as we passed, a couple of men I recognized from the Green Forward group helping him.

Jean slowed, so we could speak.

"We're putting together supply kits," Mali said. "Do you need any out your way?"

"We need dozens," Jean said, "but most of our able-bodied members are tied up on other projects. I don't think I can send anyone to help."

"We're helping each other," he said. "I'll have someone deliver them to your church, if you can pass them out."

A small miracle, I thought, as we drove away.

"Look at the steeple off the Baptist church," Jean said. "It's on Major Wilson's real estate office."

"Now that's a storm with a sense of irony."

Jean wanted to stop at the Lakeside Motel to check on little Asa and see what we might do to help. I hoped to confirm there was room for me and Chris for the next few weeks.

"Shhh," Pearl said as we walked into the office. "I just got him to sleep." Asa lay in a portable crib, and his grandmother stood behind the counter in the spot where I met her when I moved to Green, an attractive African American woman who had a spirit as beautiful as her elegant face.

She left the door ajar as we stepped outside and settled into plastic Adirondack chairs that dotted the premises. Pearl put the baby monitor on her chair arm.

"We can't stay long," I said, my mind unable to settle on one thing for more than a few minutes.

"I was so very sad to hear about Levi," Jean said.

I felt ashamed and moved to the arm of Pearl's chair. "I am, too."

"It's been one of the hardest things we've ever gone through," Pearl said. "Levi was an extraordinary gentleman. Marcus and I had come to think of him as family. It has hit Kevin especially hard, knowing he loved Asa so dearly."

"Have you talked to her lately?" I asked.

"She can't leave the hospital," Pearl said, "but she sent word to bring Asa over this morning. She needed to see with her own eyes that he was OK. It was a miracle, really. His Papa Levi saved his life."

A miracle.

"We'll head over to the hospital and check on Kevin," I said. "Does she need food or anything?"

"Terrence took her lunch before heading back out to help Marcus. He's a fine man, and the Lord sent him along at the right time."

Jean and I made it to the hospital on the newer side of town after a series of detours that included bypassing police roadblocks, tree limbs, and an odd assortment of items scattered here and there. The traffic crawled, a combination of service vehicles and what looked like curiosity seekers, many taking pictures.

A volunteer officer tried to keep us from turning down a residential street, an exasperated look on his face and sweat on his forehead.

"Clergy," Jean said.

"Press," I said.

He took a closer look. "Go on through, but watch out for debris in the street."

"Don't these rubberneckers have anything else to do?" I asked Jean. "They could be helping instead of getting in the way."

"People are drawn to tragedy," she said. "They hear so many bad reports that it's hard for them to listen to good news. Many of these cars carry people who are thinking that were it not for the grace of God, it could have been them."

"Do you have to be nice about everything?"

"I'm just glad I have my own parking place at the hospital," she said.

As she predicted, the hospital lot was full and the lobby had been transformed into a camp with bedding and miscellaneous clothing strewn everywhere. People huddled in clusters, some crying and others glued to the generator-powered television.

"I'll stop here for a while," Jean said. "It looks like there's a mighty need for prayer in this room."

I found Kevin in a discussion with a family at a nurse's station on the second floor. Her lab coat was spotless and her beautiful dark hair pulled back. She held up a finger. "One moment, Lois," she said. Her eyes looked tired, and her voice sounded raw.

Sitting in a chair in a nearby waiting room, I watched a steady stream of patients, medical personnel, and visitors come by. Instead of a gloomy atmosphere, there was a brisk efficiency about everyone, almost matter-of-fact.

"Lois, is that you?" A woman's weak voice greeted me, and I turned to see Anna Grace being wheeled down the hall on a gurney by a young woman and man with "Hospital Volunteer" vests on.

"Anna Grace!" I ran to the bed and leaned in to hug her.

"Careful, ma'am," the man said.

"Nonsense," my food correspondent said. "I need a hug more than I need medicine."

"How are you?" I embraced her.

"Much better," she said. "They're moving me to another room so they can take care of those who aren't doing as well. Your wedding saved my life."

"Saved your life? You had a heart attack," I said.

"My house was demolished," she said. "I would have been on the couch reading a cookbook and blown away right along with it. It's a miracle."

A miracle.

"I never did get a piece of that wedding cake, though," she said. "Was it too dry?"

I thought about it for a moment. "I don't know. I never got a piece either."

"I'll make you another one," she said, "when I get out of this place."

"Get well," I called as they wheeled her down the room, narrowly avoiding a metal trash can and a line of cots that had been set up in the hall.

Each time Kevin tried to walk over to me, someone demanded her attention with a form to sign, a tearful exchange of words, an apparent discussion of one medication over another. I finally gently tugged on her arm.

"Come with me, friend. Just for a few minutes."

"I can't, Lois. Everyone needs something. I can't desert them."

"I see your partner down the hall," I said, "and there are two nurses behind you. You're not going to be a bit of use if you keel over from exhaustion."

I pulled harder on her arm. "Let me buy you a cup of coffee."

"We won't be able to talk in the cafeteria," she said. "People even follow me into the bathroom."

"Let's try this then." I opened the door to a small supply closet. "Charmingly intimate, don't you think?" I wanted so much to bring a smile to her face.

She sank onto the hard tile as though it were a pillow-top mattress and propped her head against a shelf full of white sheets. I sat next to her.

"Have you seen Asa?" she asked.

"He was sound asleep, and your mother said he didn't realize anything was wrong. He looked adorable, as usual."

"That's a blessing. He'll learn soon enough how hard life is."

Her tone sounded bitter, reminding me of the days when bureaucracy nearly kept her from adopting Asa.

"Asa has a good life." I scooted closer. She leaned her head on my shoulder.

"His mother and sisters died in a house fire that

nearly took his life and critically injured his grandfather. Now that dear man has been killed brutally in a tornado. Doesn't sound that good to me."

"He has a loving mother who will always take care of him, a mother who is saving lives today."

"I should have taken him to the wedding with me," she said, a tear rolling down her face. "He would have been safe. Instead I'm out on a date while my baby nearly gets killed."

"Kevin, you had no way of knowing."

"Did you hear what happened when Terrence found Levi, right before he died?"

I shook my head.

"Levi raised his arm, pointed toward the bathroom, and said 'Asa?' Terrence assured him Asa was fine, and Papa Levi said, 'Going home.' And he died."

Kevin's lip trembled, and I hugged her with the tight grip of friendship. "He was at peace because Asa is in the best hands," I said.

"I've got to get back to work." She rose with a groan. "I saw the extra edition of the *Item*. Very impressive. The how-to-get-help piece provided a big service, and we've had at least two dozen medical volunteers come to town in response to your Internet postings."

We stood close and both cried for a moment. "Tell Mama I'll try to get home in the morning. I need to rock my baby."

"You know he'll want you to run around the yard with him," I said.

Someone knocked on the door and opened it tentatively. "Dr. Kevin, are you in there?" a woman's voice said. "We need you in Room 207."

Jean and I stopped at the command center next. Emergency vehicles from nearby towns and parishes and media vans filled the courthouse parking lot.

The basement was packed, and I noticed Linda arguing with the police chief, a rugged-looking man in his forties, near the front of the room. The air almost crackled around them. An unknown person was working on an *Item* laptop at the desk in the back of the room.

"I'm going to talk to Eva," Jean said. "Then I'll head back to the church to figure out the next step."

"If you run into Chris again, tell him I'm doing fine. Please remind him to check on Joe Sepulvado, the produce guy. We haven't had a chance to get by their travel trailer."

A small frown crossed her face. "Now that you mention it, I haven't seen Joe," she said, adding his name to a long list in her hand, some checked off, a dozen with question marks.

I approached Linda and the chief, their voices low but angry. "Everything OK?" I asked.

"No," Linda said.

"Yes," Doug said at the same time.

"He doesn't want to release the names of the confirmed dead," Linda said. "Nor those who are missing. We can help locate people if he'll work with us."

"People have a right to hear this personally," the chief said, "not through the media."

"Wouldn't you rather they know than be left to wonder and worry?" Linda asked.

Doug mumbled something under his breath.

"He says if he gives them to us, he has to give them to everyone," Linda said. "He doesn't trust the others to handle this with sympathy."

"The outside media's sensationalizing this for their own gain," Doug said. "Some of them act excited when they learn another lurid tidbit. I can't risk letting them have the names."

"Chief, they'll get them through you or they'll piece them together," I said. "If they make a list, they're sure to get names wrong. Think how tragic that could be."

"If I never see another reporter that will be all right with me," he muttered. "Present company included." And he stalked off.

"That went well," I said.

"He'll come around," Linda said. "Cops like to be in control. This is about as out of control as you can be."

"I didn't think I had anything in common with that man, but I feel the same way."

Within a few minutes, the chief slipped Linda the updated list of confirmed dead and those missing. "I'll give you a twenty-minute head start," he said. "Then it goes to everyone. And this better remain between us."

After making a copy of the names, I got into a fight with an out-of-town reporter sitting at what was now called the media desk, and I thought of physically pushing her out of the chair.

"We need to work here," I said.

"What does it look like I'm doing, planning a vacation?" she asked, her eyes on the screen of my computer.

I reached over her shoulder, hit save, and snapped the computer shut. "That's my laptop," I said.

She looked up at me with what could only be described as fury. Her mouth opened, and I waited for the showdown.

"Lois?" her voice sounded incredulous. "Lois Barker?"

"Lois Craig." I searched through my scrambled brain for an idea of who this woman was. She was a few years younger than me and had on a designer watch, chic glasses, and an expensive shirt I recognized from a catalog. Her shoulder-length hair was pushed back by a leather headband.

"Gina Stonecash. Post Media News Service. We met at that meeting on education coverage right before you left the company."

"Gina." I remembered a room full of Gina clones, all eager to show the corporate V.P. how much they knew. "What in the world are you doing here?"

"Covering the biggest breaking news story in the country," she said. "You, too?"

"You might say that. I own the local newspaper."

"You're that tough lady journalist everyone's talking about?" Gina asked, her eyes wide.

"Lois?" Linda walked up behind me and nudged me. "The clock's running. I need the computer."

"Gina, let me introduce you to a terrific reporter, Linda Murphy. Would you like to walk over and see our newsroom?"

Linda slipped into the chair almost before Gina was out of it, and I waved to Jean and Eva as we walked out. Heading across the street, I smiled to think that we were beating the competition, which included the corporation I used to work for.

"You're whipping everyone with online updates," Gina said. "Not to mention those community correspondents. Their perspective is a pleasure to read. Where in the world do you come up with those people? Zach's already nagging me to set up a national network like that."

"Zach? As in my former boss? The editor in Dayton?"

"Former editor. He got promoted to corporate,

works in D.C. now. Funny that he didn't mention you were down here."

"We didn't part on the best of terms." I led her through the labyrinth of the parking lot.

"Ta da," I said, with more than a hint of pride. "*The Green News-Item.*"

"You own this? For real?"

"Mostly for real. The bank has a share, and the employees are co-owners. But I get to sign the checks."

"I vaguely remember something about this," Gina said. "Didn't that managing editor who died leave it to you?"

"My friend Ed. He planned to retire down here and run it, but he lost a fight with leukemia. I had no intention of moving to rural North Louisiana, but apparently God had other plans."

"God?" Gina said. "As I recall, you used to be a devoted follower of Post Media. There's life outside the corporate grind?"

"Miracle of miracles, there is. Green is a great place to live."

"Did you say earlier that your name is Lois Craig now?" She glanced at my hand. "When did you get married?"

"Last night."

8

Mildred Kersh is in desperate need
of someone to work on her hair before
her brother-in-law's funeral service day
after tomorrow. "My cousin's granddaughter
is going to cosmetology school and she
wanted to give me a new look last week,"
Milly said. "It is not at all what I
had in mind. If you know of anyone
who might be able to do something with
this mess, please let me know."
—*The Green News-Item*

Chris and I set up housekeeping in Room Eight, the very room I had stayed in when I moved to Green.

"Shall I carry you over the threshold?" he asked with an exhausted smile as we took our suitcases into the room. On a chilly evening two years ago, I had walked into the room, alone and lost, begging my friend Marti by phone to let me come home.

Standing next to my beloved husband, I felt a sliver of relief from the grief of the past twenty-four hours.

Before I could step further into the room, Chris embraced me. "What a day," he said. "How are you holding up?"

111

I jerked away. "Lights!" I shouted. "Chris, the lights are coming on." Sure enough, as we stood in the clean old motel room, the electricity came on. People overflowed from the handful of other rooms, yelling, and we rushed outside.

Iris Jo, Stan, and Pearl had been sitting outside, visiting, when we drove up, Asa playing nearby. Holly Beth, rescued from the newspaper by Iris, was running around, barking, trying to get someone to pay attention to her.

"Praise the Lord," Mr. Marcus said. Little Asa toddled behind him and clapped his hands, clearly aware that something good was happening.

An elusive feeling of a new kind of normalcy washed over me. Electricity and a honeymoon with my new extended family had not been on my list of blessings yesterday.

"I'd better go see if we got power at the paper," Stan said, standing up. He leaned over and gave Iris a sweet, long kiss, so potent and unexpected that it made me want to look away. "Don't stay up too late. You're not back to full strength yet."

"Yes, sir," she said quietly and reached up for another quick kiss.

"Kiss, kiss, bye, bye," Asa Corinthian said, tugging on Stan's pants leg, and everyone burst out laughing.

Chris picked the boy up and held him up, flying like an airplane, and Asa pointed in the distance. "Mama car," he squealed. "Mama car!"

He had spotted Kevin's SUV long before the rest of us and was waving wildly. "Mama, mama," he called.

Kevin ran from the vehicle, not even taking time to shut the door. "Asa, baby," she said, taking him from Chris and squeezing him in a hug.

"Stuck," Asa said, squirming from her grip, and we laughed again.

"I'm sorry, little guy," Kevin said. "Mama missed you so much."

"Puppy," Asa said. "See puppy."

"Upstaged by Holly Beth," I said. "Happens to me all the time."

"Have you had supper?" Kevin's mother asked.

"Terrence brought food before heading back to Alexandria," she said. "I want to visit for a minute, tuck my son in, and have a bath. Then, back to work."

"You're not going back to the hospital tonight, are you?" Pearl asked, her voice a mix of disapproval and disappointment.

"I have to, Mama," she said. "We've got more patients than physicians."

"When is that handsome lawyer coming back to town?" Pearl asked. "He was a big help to us today."

"I don't know," Kevin said. "He's got a lot on his plate, and so do I." She promptly changed the subject.

For the next few minutes, we all chatted,

everyone hungry for news about neighbors, seeking any positive tidbit.

"Anna Grace should be home by the middle of the week," Kevin said. "She wanted me to let you know."

"Lois and I have some good news about Mannix," Chris said. "He's going to pull through. He's lost a leg, but he ate today. When I stopped by the vet's, I think he was asking for Lois." He reached over and squeezed my hand.

"I ran into a journalism colleague from my old life today," I said. "She was pretty darned impressed with the way we do things down here in Green. My old boss wants to try our techniques."

"So, you're going to be famous?" Iris Jo said with a smile.

"Probably not, but I'm going to soak this up while I can."

"I'm ready to soak up some hot water," Kevin said, "and a little snuggling time with my boy."

I glanced at Chris. "Not a bad idea."

The next few days fell into a new kind of routine. Our schedule included mooching supper off someone and getting in a few more hours of work, newspaper on my end, repairs on Chris's. When we finally headed to the Lakeside, the cozy room was a welcome retreat, a romantic cocoon in the midst of chaos.

Electricity was back on in about three-fourths of

114

town, a reflection of the herculean efforts of utility workers who dotted every light pole in the area. "Let There Be Light," read the main headline on Tuesday. "Power restored to portions of Green." The subhead was grimmer: "Have You Seen These People? Search Continues for Lost Residents."

The list of the dead on the front window was somber, and residents came by in droves to look over the names. Molly recommended we add names of the missing, and she and Katy painted those under the giant words "Not Heard From Yet," joyfully putting a line through a name when the person turned up.

"I am over in Coushatta at my sister's," one woman said, calling the command center.

"That family is out of town for spring break," came another report.

Slowly the list dwindled to fewer than a half dozen, including the discovery of a couple, both injured but taken to two out-of-town hospitals. Two names did not go away. Mr. and Mrs. Joe Sepulvado, poor immigrants from Mexico who lived in an old travel trailer not too far from my house. Or what used to be my house.

Joe grew produce and recycled cans to send money to his family, attended the Spanish service at Grace Chapel, and had been unjustly accused of arson at the paper last year. I winced when I thought of how his life had nearly been ruined by

115

Chuck McCuller, who started the fires and gloated when Joe was arrested.

Chris and I visited the Sepulvados in the fall so I could apologize for not clearing his name sooner, and we had committed as a couple to try to help them out in the months ahead. I had expected to invite them over to our house for dinner, not search the countryside for them.

"We have to look again," I told Chris when he stopped to pick me up for supper on Wednesday.

"Sweetheart, I've looked for them every day this week," he said, a husky sound in his throat, as though a frog had lodged there. "Their trailer is turned over on its side, but they are nowhere to be found."

"Maybe someone came by and picked them up."

"Possibly," Chris said.

"Could they have gotten scared and somehow gone back to Mexico?"

"I doubt it, but there's so much confusion, anything could happen."

"Have you checked at the hospital?"

"You asked me that last night. I've checked three times and I asked Kevin when I saw her leaving for work this morning."

My attitude toward the visiting press had softened as the week wore on, and I decided to seek their help. Reporters came and went in our building, using the bathroom, grabbing a cup of coffee, and chatting; and I told them about the

Sepulvados, asking them to be on the lookout for any news that might help us find them.

A photographer from New Orleans found Mrs. Sepulvado's body while taking pictures near where my house had sat on Route Two. The body was under a sheet of tin and partially covered by tree limbs. A group of volunteers from Grace Chapel intensified the search for Joe, finding not so much as a clue.

For the first time in several days, I wept. Hard, angry tears. The Sepulvados had sacrificed to provide for their family and to have a better life. I couldn't understand why such bad things had happened to so many good people.

If I had had more time, I would have set off for Pastor Jean's to rant and ask for counsel, but we were all going in so many directions that I simply buried it, feeling a cold, hard knot growing inside me.

That evening I asked Chris to drive me to my old house site, the first time I had been there since the night of the storm. Less than a week had passed, but it felt like a lifetime. Several people, including other reporters, had asked me about it, but I had put off going back.

"I'm way too busy for that, and there's nothing to see," I said to Gina, who seemed to have settled in Green for the long haul, renting a room in the newer motel on the edge of town.

When Chris picked me up, Katy and Molly and

Tammy were in the newsroom, along with a camera crew from a Shreveport television station and a wire service reporter from Little Rock, who had swapped places with a reporter from Houston.

"Let us go with you," the journalists said. "We'll document your reaction. It'll be a great story."

"It's too personal," I said hesitantly, realizing how pushy I had been in the past.

"Absolutely not," Chris said. "Lois has been through too much this week. You can hear about it later." A few months ago his words would have irritated me, as though he were trying to take over my life or "be the boss of me," as Tammy liked to say. Today they made me feel cared for.

We went by my in-laws' house, in pretty decent shape compared to many homes nearby. Markey and Kramer ran and got into the back of the pickup as soon as we pulled up, and Mannix, lying on a blanket on the porch, whined and tried to stand.

Chris laid him on the front seat, gingerly placing his weight away from the bandage where his leg had been severed. I chatted with Miss Estelle and Mr. Hugh and pried Holly away from my father-in-law, who had kept her for the past couple of days.

When we got to my home place, Kramer and Markey dashed off, as though they had been let out of prison after several decades, and then came back to the truck, barking for Mannix. Chris put him on the blanket on the ground, and Mannix tried to stand up, yelped, and lay back down. The two other dogs whimpered as though they were wounded and wandered off, sniffing every inch of the ground.

I placed Holly Beth down beside Mannix. When I looked back minutes later, she was snuggled up against him, sound asleep. The bigger dog was intently watching the area, but did not try to get up.

Chris and I walked around the house, almost as though it still sat there. The memory of it was so real I felt as though I might climb the steps and go in the side door, throw my keys on the table as I had done a thousand times, and flop down in my favorite chair with a book.

Despite the devastation, many of the old plants bloomed, even though they were beaten down from wind, rain, and hail. The pink dogwood still stood, many blooms open, almost like a poem or prayer in the front yard.

Chris wrapped his arms around my waist from behind, and we stood facing the tree.

"This makes me homesick," I said. "Where are we going to live?"

"Where do you want to live?"

"Here. But I've grown accustomed to a roof over my head."

"We'd have to build," Chris said. "Neither one of us is up to that decision right now."

119

"I can't imagine living anywhere other than Route Two," I said, "even though I dreamed about living on the lake when I first came to Green."

An odd look passed over his face. "Let's give it a few days."

On the drive back to town, I asked Chris to go the long way, past his catfish ponds, taken over by his brothers since the storm, and down around the crossroads where a small grocery store and abandoned church sat.

"Right over there is where I first saw you," I said, petting Mannix.

"I remember it well," Chris said.

"I was talking to Mannix. Remember? He came running out barking, and I was afraid of him and got mud on my new shoes?"

"Oh, I remember," Chris said. "I wondered how a good-looking city girl got so lost, and then I walked into church and you were sitting there in those muddy shoes. I thanked God right on the spot."

"You did not. You were listening to Iris and barely looked at me."

"Oh, honey, I looked all right," he said, reaching over Mannix to pat my knee. "It took me a while to get up the nerve to talk to you."

"Our marriage sure has had a rough start," I said.

He pulled over to the side of the road and turned to me. "Do you know how much harder this would have been if you weren't my wife? You make it bearable."

"Ditto," I said, nearly undone by the tenderness in his eyes.

As we meandered on country roads to Estelle and Hugh's house, Chris pointed out oddities he'd seen the past few days.

"Those people," he said, pointing to a caved-in house, "lost everything but the kitchen sink . . . and the woman's wedding ring was lying on the sink, right where she left it.

"That man had driven to the hardware store to buy a saw blade. His mobile home rolled several times. He says a five-dollar tool saved his life."

"Think about Route Two," I said. "That twister knocked the biggest oak in the parish into Iris Jo's house, skipped across the road, blew away my house but hardly touched my trees, ruined the church . . . yet missed Maria's trailer."

"It seems like a wild animal on a rampage," Chris said.

"I learned something else about tornadoes, too," I said.

"What's that?"

"They honestly do sound like a train."

Chris laughed and turned down a rutted dirt road. "While we're out this way, I'll run you by that house Maria and the boys used to rent. You're not going to believe it. One of my players lives near there, too. I'd like to see how he's doing."

121

We slowly made our way toward a grove of trees. Mannix whimpered when we hit an especially big bump, and I petted his head.

"Sorry, guy," Chris said. "I'm trying to make this as easy on you as I know how."

We stopped at the first building we came to, a shotgun house that leaned at a precarious angle, and had aluminum foil over the windows and a broken soft-drink machine in the front yard. "Oh, that one took a hit," I said.

"Afraid not," Chris said. "It looked like that before the storm."

A teenaged boy came out of the house, followed by a girl of about seven and a baby in a diaper crawling across the yard. I couldn't tell if it was a boy or a girl.

"Hey, Coach," the boy said.

"Y'all all right out here, Anthony?" Chris asked.

"We're OK," the boy said, shrugging his shoulders.

"I'm hungry," the little girl said. "Do you know when we get to go back to school?"

The boy looked embarrassed but didn't say anything, just picked up the baby and settled the infant on his hip.

"Don't you have extra supplies?" I asked Chris, stricken.

"It so happens I have lots of things in here," he said. He opened the truck door and reached behind the seat to pull out an emergency food kit from the

Methodist church and a sack of groceries his mother had given us, with cheese and crackers, oranges, and a big jar of applesauce. "This might help for today. I'll be out this way in the next couple of days and I'll have more then."

"Thanks, sir," the boy said, handing the baby to the girl and taking the bag and box from Chris.

"That tornado hurt so many people," I said as we drove on down the little road.

"That's not storm damage," Chris said. "They depend on school meals to be fed. I don't know what the baby does. When school's out, lots of kids in this area have no food."

"How can that be?" I asked. "We've got to help them. Surely the paper and the church can come up with something."

"That's my Lois," Chris said, smiling at me. "But it'll take a lot more than a bag of groceries every now and then. You're witnessing a major problem in rural Bouef Parish."

He drove on down the dead-end road to where Maria and her sons had lived, a patch of land that nearly connected to the church's property but was accessible only by the back road. I had come here with Chris and Pastor Jean to help Maria and the children move and knew the rundown house, rented from a friend of a friend at work, had stood under the big cottonwood tree. Now a pile of boards was all that remained, except for a small shed to the side.

Chris slowly stepped out of the truck, a cue for the two dogs in the back to jump out and run around. Always gentle with Mannix, Chris once more took him from the truck. I had never been a dog person before I moved to Green, but I thought how a man treated animals said a lot about him.

"It fell down," I whispered. "You saved their lives by giving them your mobile home."

"It's a miracle," Chris said. "There's no other word for it."

With the word *miracle* hanging in the air between us, Mannix, who had been immobile since the storm, shakily got to his feet, fell down, and then stood back up on his three legs.

"Here, boy," Chris said, reaching for the animal.

Instead of moving toward Chris, Mannix took off at a slow gait, trying to get his balance. He barked loudly and whined, ignoring Kramer and Markey when they came bounding toward him. I left Holly Beth on the truck seat and hurried to catch up with him and Chris.

Chris reached for Mannix. "Come here, you big lug," he said quietly, but when he touched the dog, it turned and snapped at him, something I had never seen it do to anyone.

"It must be the pain," I said, feeling bad for Chris, who looked stunned.

Mannix kept limping forward, barking and whining, with the occasional growl thrown in, headed straight for the ramshackle shed.

"Mannix," I pleaded, "don't go near that. It looks like it could fall right on top of you. Chris, be careful."

The dog continued on, Chris on his heels, me following timidly behind.

Mannix walked right into the dark shed, over to a pile of rags on the floor, lay down, and barked even louder, then started licking the lump.

He had found Mr. Sepulvado.

"If he had stayed out there a few more hours, he would have been dead," Kevin said later that evening when we sat outside the motel.

"Are you sure he'll make it?" I asked, reaching again for Chris's hand.

"These days I'm not sure of much," Kevin said, "but he's a survivor. He's severely dehydrated and in extreme shock. Anyone else would have died three days ago."

I shook from the memory of Mr. Sepulvado, covered in fire ants and the look of death about him, the drive back to town with three of the dogs up front and me cradling Joe in the back of the truck, laid out on Mannix's blanket. The injured dog refused to leave his side and rested his chin on Mr. Sepulvado's stomach, whimpering when we hit a bump.

"How did he get there?" I asked for the tenth time since we had dropped him off at the hospital.

"Honey," Chris said gently, as though talking to

125

a demented person, "we don't know that. We suspect he was trying to find his wife and got disoriented after the storm."

"He must have found water along the way," Kevin said, "but who knows? When he regains consciousness, perhaps we'll learn more."

Pastor Jean had joined us and sat near Iris and Stan.

"He's a fine man," Jean said. "And his wife was a fine woman. I need to notify his family and set up a service for her."

"How will we tell him?" I asked, leaning into Chris.

"I'll take care of that," Pastor Jean said, rubbing a hand across her eyes, "when Kevin thinks he can handle the news."

"Mannix the three-legged dog," as he was now known, was a national hero, upstaging a helicopter visit from the governor.

The dog was then pampered, photographed, and all-but interviewed.

His story earned him an oversized care package from a major pet supply chain and a call from an agent who wanted to put him in a commercial. Mannix also brought a second horde of reporters to town, all eager to talk about the small-town newspaper owner and her miraculous dog.

Chris would look at me, smile, and roll his eyes.

9

Sam Boyce, host of Green's radio talk show Hooked on Fishing, *was questioned by police two evenings ago after a traffic snarl-up on Main Street. Witnesses said Boyce, pulling a trailer behind his pickup, was seen driving well below the speed limit, weaving from one side of the road to the other and ignoring all stop signs. A police spokeswoman said he claimed he was "trolling for a tornado, determined not to be surprised by one again."*
—The Green News-Item

The mayor summoned me to her home for lunch five days after the storm hit.

When I rang the doorbell, Sugar Marie barked, and Dub McCuller opened the door, a kitchen towel in his hand.

I took a step back.

"Come in, Miss Barker," he said. "Eva's running a few minutes late."

"It's Craig," I said, frozen to the spot. "Lois Craig."

"I forgot," he said. "Congratulations. The Craigs are good people."

The last time I had seen Dub was the night he came to my house to tell me his brother, now

127

dead, was the one who set a series of fires to run me out of town. He had apologized that night for suing me in order to regain control of the paper.

I wasn't exactly afraid of Dub, but I didn't want to have lunch with him.

Sugar Marie provided a welcome distraction, greeting me like her long-lost best buddy, but that didn't last. After sniffing and looking around, she seemed to realize I hadn't brought Holly Beth and slunk off in a pout.

"She's moody, isn't she?" Dub asked.

That could be the first thing he'd ever said that I agreed with.

"Maybe it would be better if I met the mayor downtown," I said. "We're both on tight schedules."

"She should be here any minute," Dub said. "I've got lunch ready and will leave you two to your business while I run errands."

Dub cooked lunch? Eva had mentioned the two were making amends after a long-standing misunderstanding, but I didn't realize it had come to this.

I glanced down at my shoes, intimidated not only by Dub but by Eva's white carpet. The cute hiking shoes I had bought for my honeymoon had been muddy since Sunday, and I slipped them off before walking in.

Dub chuckled. "Eva's frighteningly neat, isn't she?" he asked. "I set a glass on the table without a coaster the other day, and she politely reminded me it wasn't a good idea."

Chitchat from this sixty-ish man, wearing jeans and an LSU polo shirt, was painful. I had dealt with him and Chuck after my friend Ed died and left the paper—and a large bank note—to me. I had fought the brothers, the Big Boys, for most of last year. No way was I going to forgive him for all of that at a little luncheon.

"I make you uneasy," Dub said, guiding me into the foyer of the house. "I hope you know how sorry I am about everything. I made so many mistakes. I'm trying to make things right with a lot of people."

"This is awkward," I said. "I've been working eighteen-hour days, my house blew away, and I don't have the energy for this conversation. Tell the mayor I'll catch up with her later."

As I opened the door, Eva whipped into the driveway in her new Cadillac so fast that I thought she might hit the garage door.

"Excuse me," Dub said, and walked through the living room and into the kitchen to greet Eva. I could hear the two talking in low tones, and heard a door close. I walked into the kitchen, feeling like a child who had thrown a fit.

Eva put her purse on the bar and picked up Sugar Marie. The mayor had perfected the leader-in-time-of-crisis look and wore tan linen slacks and a matching tunic, with a big, colorful scarf draped around her shoulders. If I had tried a similar outfit, I would have looked like a crone in a movie, the wicked woman who delivers poison apples to children. She looked calm and determined.

"So I hear you don't care for my choice of housekeepers?" she said.

I moved over to hug her, keeping a close eye on Sugar Marie. "Dub makes me uncomfortable," I said. "He did so much damage."

"Undeniably," she said. "It's your choice whether you forgive him or not. I know he is committed to being a better man."

Through the window over the sink, as she spoke, I saw Dub back out of the garage.

"He *parks* in your garage? Is he living here?" I blurted.

Eva's demeanor shifted into pure irritation, a rare look for her in any situation.

"Because you're a friend, I assume those questions were not meant to be insulting," Eva said. "He's helped out since the storm, taken care of Sugar Marie, done repairs . . . now that I think about it, taken care of me when everyone else in town is asking something of me. Of course he doesn't live here, but I thought it might keep gossip down if his truck wasn't parked out front."

"I'm sorry, Eva. I was rude. Dub caught me off guard."

"Enough of that," she waved her hand as though

dismissing the topic from the room. "We won't have much time before reporters start hounding me or an unhappy citizen comes looking for me. Serve your plate and let's get to work."

"To work?" I asked, dishing up soup and salad into heavy white pottery dishes. I wondered on which of her many travels the mayor had found those.

"I need your brain," she said, escorting me into the dining room with two placemats, silverware, and water glasses in place.

"My brain?" At that moment it seemed fairly useless.

"I hoped we might have a quick private lunch and come up with a plan," Eva said.

"A plan?"

"Are you all right?" she asked.

I sipped ice-cold water from a crystal glass. "I can't tell if I'm acting crazy because I ran into Dub or because I'm sitting down to eat lunch at a nice table in a beautiful home."

Eva laughed, and I relaxed.

"Lois, it hit me yesterday that it's time to quit reacting and respond. We've made it past the crisis and we have to look at the future."

"Made it past the crisis?" I nearly choked on an almond in the salad. "Have you driven around town lately? Green is nothing but crisis."

"That's not the answer I'm looking for," Eva said, laying her spoon down. "I invited you here because I know you won't wallow in self-pity. We don't have time for that. We're facing major issues in Green, and I need help in deciding what to do next."

"Eva," I said, giving up the pretense of eating, "we're less than a week into this. Is that enough time to know what to do next? Most people can barely put one foot in front of the other."

"If we don't get proactive here, Green may never come out of this."

My mayor, a woman I admired greatly, had used the word *proactive*. I *hated* the word *proactive*. To make matters worse, I liked self-pity and was hoping to get a lot of mileage out of it during the next few weeks at least. I was exhausted. I wanted to finish my lunch, which, I had to hand it to Dub, was quite tasty. Then I would like to lie down on Eva's fancy brocade couch and take a nap, pulling that cashmere throw she bought in Italy over me.

Looking in the mayor's eyes, I knew a nap was not in my future.

"Do you have any strong coffee?" I asked.

"Dub turned it on right before you ran him off," she said with a smile. "Finish your lunch while I get you a cup."

When she returned, she not only had the coffeepot but a stack of white note cards and a large black marker.

"Are we going to make flash cards?" I asked.

"In a manner of speaking," she said. "We've got

to flash forward and think of who is going to come out of the woodwork and what they're going to want, how we're going to meet real needs, and keep from doing the wrong thing."

"We might as well add unintended consequences and multiply the time and money it's going to take to get things done," I said.

"You're finally getting my point," Eva said. "We had a solid plan to deal with a disaster, and, with the *Item*'s help, we've done a pretty good job with rescue. The true test is going to be recovery."

"Why not have a town meeting? Ask for input," I said.

"Clearly we're going to do that, but I wonder if there are other steps we need to take first. You're the only one I can think of who can help pull this together. You see the big picture, and you have enough of an outsider's perspective to analyze more clearly."

Her reference to my outsider's perspective stung. I felt like a lifelong resident—even if I didn't have a house at the moment.

"Hand me that marker," I said, and wrote the word *future* in large letters on one card and *tradition* on the next.

"Good point," Eva murmured. "We will have to tie the future to the past or everyone will be contrary."

"Change is next," I said. "Hopefully the storm

blew away Green's resistance to change."

"I wouldn't count on it," Eva said. "We're going to do things differently, though."

"Urgency," I added. "We must have a sense of urgency. We don't have time to waste."

"But that will make people nervous," she said. "Maybe the word *steady* is better. People need to be motivated to do what needs to be done, but they won't want to feel rushed."

For the next forty-five minutes, we wrote word after word and discussed idea after idea, until a sketchy scenario emerged.

"Let's get the Green Forward group together tomorrow after the paper comes out," Eva said, "and see what they want to add."

Dub drove up as I was leaving and took a ladder and toolbox out of his truck. Across the street, a youth work crew with bright First Baptist Church T-shirts piled branches on the street. A couple of houses down I saw a woman delivering one of Pastor Mali's supply packages.

Sitting in my car, I pulled out the stack of cards and added one more word.

Compassion.

Wearing a mongrammed pullover, Gina was in the newsroom the next afternoon, and I invited her to attend the Green Forward meeting.

"This is a great group," I said. "They care passionately about making Green a better place to live. You'll get a good look at what small-town life is like."

Big mistake on my part.

The meeting, held in the newspaper conference room, started with an argument. Everyone was tired and wanted to get to the point. My desire for compassion lasted about five minutes.

The Cotton Boll Café, which usually provided food for the group, was swamped with orders from volunteers and those in need, and Iris came up with a bag of Linda's stale pretzels and lukewarm bottled water from the newsroom.

"We want to rebuild for the future while holding on to the traditions of the past," I said, opening the meeting. What had seemed poetic yesterday at lunch sounded contrived today.

"We're pushing this," retorted one of the downtown business owners. "We're trying to get things up and running, and you want us to talk about the future. We haven't even got all the dead buried yet."

"People aren't ready to look ahead," Pastor Mali, always a supporter of my ideas, said. "They're hurting. They need food and water, not strategies."

"We're not going to overlook their basic needs," I said, frustration flowing out of every pore in my body.

"With all respect, I believe Lois is saying that food and water are part of the strategies," Eva said. "We have immediate needs to meet and must be ready for what people will need in a week or two, then a month, and on down the line."

The mayor was trying to smooth things over for me. I hoped Gina hadn't noticed.

"I sort of see what you mean," the owner of an auto mechanic shop on the south side of town said. "With the new highway under construction, this could be the right time for businesses like mine to move."

"Move?" Rose, who had taken the week off from her postal job, asked. "What do you mean 'move'?"

"If I'm going to have to start over, I might as well do it now rather than later," he said. "I've been scoping out locations."

"That's one of the issues this group needs to take a stand on," the mayor said. "I'm hearing from lots of businesses who plan to relocate. We need to discuss zoning challenges."

"Not to argue with you, Mayor," said banker Jerry, who loved nothing better than to argue with her, "but zoning could kill this town. We've got to help people earn a living and we can't be saying no every time they turn around."

I wondered if he was already shaping his campaign message for the next election, but what he said made sense. It also troubled me.

"We have to find a happy medium," Rose said. "Small businesses were barely holding on as it was. But if we let people build anywhere and everywhere, this town will look like a junkyard."

Rose as a city planner? She juggled her mail route and antique mall—and exhibited that rare combination of common sense and good ideas.

"Ultimately, the town must decide what it wants to be," said Becca, owner of the flower and gift shop who had done such a spectacular job on my wedding. "Will we be quaint and charming, the way tourists want, or another little southern town that dried up?"

"I'd say it's every man for himself at this point," a businessman grumbled.

"I'm not going to jump through hoops to please some bureaucrat," said the auto repair guy.

"Depends on how much money that bureaucrat has," Jerry said with a laugh, nudging the fellow next to him.

"We also need to consider environmental issues," I said.

The word *environmental* might as well have been a bomb going off.

Nearly everyone in the room started talking at once, and I was tempted to get under the table. "Green is an old town. When buildings are rebuilt, we might as well take advantage of new technology," I said. "We can become a more energy efficient town and live up to our name. Green will be green."

"Green will be in the red," the banker said. "Do

you know how expensive all that newfangled low-energy stuff is? That tornado might as well have wiped us right off the map if that's the direction we go."

"What do you mean we're an old town?" another business owner asked. "If you felt that way, why did you fight to keep the newspaper? You could have left it a family business with people who appreciate Green."

"I love Green," I said and took a breath to continue, but noticed Rose slightly shaking her head.

"We won't figure this out today," Rose said. "We need to commit to work together, not fight."

While we talked, Linda took notes and asked the occasional follow-up question. I noticed Gina, sitting away from the table, also scribbling away.

"You're not planning to put this in the paper, are you?" the banker asked.

"Yes, sir, I expect we will," Linda said, looking at me with a question in her eyes.

"Who is that woman over there?" he asked. "We didn't invite out-of-towners to this meeting."

"This is my former colleague, Gina Stonecash, from Washington," I said. "She's done a fine job in getting the word about Green out around the country."

"Thank you for that," Pastor Mali said.

"These meetings are off-the-record," Jerry said.

"We don't need this spread around till the time is right."

"The time is right, if you ask me," Rose said. "People need to know what they're up against."

"Let people do whatever they want, wherever they want," the banker said. "Otherwise, by the time the highway bypass is finished, there won't be anything to bypass."

"We will work together to rebuild," Mayor Eva said. "Or we will watch Green fall apart."

"I've wasted too much time in this meeting," one business owner said. "I have real work to do."

"Me too," said another.

Before I could say "adjourned," most of the crowd had scattered.

"Lois, do you have a few minutes for an interview?" Gina asked. "I'd like to do a piece on the battle to rebuild and how the newspaper is a community leader."

I groaned. "Gina—"

She had the look I had used on sources many times in the past. One way or the other, a story would be written. Maybe I could do damage control.

"Sure," I said. "I'll meet you in the newsroom in ten minutes."

As she walked out, I tugged on one of the heavy chairs and sat down next to the mayor who was text messaging and going through e-mail on her phone.

"I think we gave the fine leaders of Green a little too much credit, Eva, when we decided it was time for recovery."

"We need to recover all right," Linda said, walking out of the room. "From this meeting."

Right then I remembered that for the first time since the group had begun, we had neglected to open with a prayer.

10

Myrtie Johnson could teach us all a thing or two about hospitality. When riffraff preying on storm victims broke into her house over the weekend, she offered them a cup of coffee and invited them to church. "I knew they were hurting like the rest of us," she said. She reports she was not very happy, however, when they took her new flat-screen TV.
—The Green News-Item

My one-week wedding anniversary had arrived. It felt like a decade had passed.

"I have a gift for you," Chris said as we sat on the patio at the Lakeside Motel drinking coffee, the morning air cool, the sun barely up. These chats were precious, rare times alone with Chris when we weren't completely worn out.

"How in the world could you have gotten me a gift?" I reached over and grabbed his left hand, rubbing his wedding band. "You've been volunteering around the clock, and there are hardly any stores open." I paused and smiled. "You got me something at the Dollar Hut, didn't you? That pair of scissors I wanted."

Since the house had blown away, I had scrounged for the most basic items. Every time I turned around I needed something I didn't have, an annoying feeling that often led to melancholy.

"Give a guy a little more credit than that," he said. "How about a kiss?"

"Now that's a gift I can get into," I said, kissing him.

"I'll be right back," he said.

He opened the door to his pickup, which creaked like the hinge was about to break, and pulled out a wadded up towel.

"Is that one of my towels?" I asked. "From the house?"

"Found it two hundred yards away from the house site," he said. "There's something in it for you."

I unwrapped the towel to find a piece of my green pottery collection, a gift from Chris when he thought I was leaving town. A pitcher, it had belonged to his grandmother and had been made on Route Two. This was by far the most prized of all the pieces I had collected through the years.

"It's in perfect condition." My voice trembled. "How is that possible?"

141

"It reminds me of my wife," he said. "Strong and beautiful."

"You're trying to make me cry, aren't you?"

"I hoped it would bring a smile to your face," he said.

"I guess I should go out there and look around again," I said. "But it makes me sad to think about it."

"That pottery's about the only thing worth saving out there. Most everything was either broken or got ruined by the rain."

"This is a treasure." I held up the piece of pottery. "Some things do last forever."

"Like us," he said.

"Like us."

At the paper an hour later, I ushered the staff to my office.

"It's been a week today," I said. "You all need a break."

"Your marriage has been a real whirlwind," Tammy said, one of a near constant string of jokes.

"She's blown away by your remarks," Katy said.

Wedding plus tornado seemed to equal humor material in most people's minds. I also knew that the jokes took our minds off the pain.

"The insane hours you're working are getting to you," I said. "You need time off."

"We want to do what we've been doing," Alex said. "Beating the pants off the competition and making a name for *The Green News-Item*."

"Don't you mean making a name for yourself?" Katy asked. "I've seen you talking to those people from Baton Rouge and New Orleans."

"Like you've been talking to all those television people?" Alex shot back. "Maybe you're thinking newspapers aren't good enough for you any more."

"Alex, Katy. Stop. Now."

"Whatever we do, we've got to keep the bank balance in mind," Iris said. "The tornado has cost us a lot of money."

"I hoped we could do a special keepsake edition in a month or so," Tammy said. "Combine reader contributions with the best of our material."

"I might be able to sell advertising for that," Linda said. "Businesses have to spread the word that they're alive and well. Plus we have all the roofing contractors and insurance companies and contractors hitting town."

"At some point . . ." I said and had to clear my throat, the words hung there. "At some point, we have to talk about long-term plans."

I looked around the room and fidgeted with my wedding ring.

"Katy and Molly are going off to college," I said. "That's only four months or so. Tammy's getting married. We haven't said a word about Tom."

A look of sadness crossed the faces of the group as I moved my eyes around the table.

143

"We never even got to say good-bye to him," Katy said. "Life's been such a zoo that it doesn't seem real."

"I keep thinking he'll come back and need a word for a puzzle or be making a sculpture out of toothpicks or another of his weird projects," Linda said.

"Or fussing at me for using 'affect' instead of 'effect,'" Alex said.

"Maybe we could have a service for him," Iris Jo said.

"Tom would hate a funeral," Molly said. "He'd roll over in his—" She stopped when she realized what she was saying.

"Lois, you want us to take a break from the newsroom today, right?" Katy asked.

"No question."

"What if we had a party for Tom? He liked our get-togethers out at your house."

"I don't have a house. I guess we could do it at the Lakeside." At times I forgot that the house was gone. A couple of evenings I had started driving that way after work before remembering that I lived at a motel. At other times the loss was right at the surface.

"Why not out where your house was?" Katy asked.

I turned to Iris. "Is this too weird? Is it too soon?"

"Tom liked weird," she said with her gentle smile.

144

"It can be a modified memorial service," Linda said. "It's a beautiful time of year to be outdoors."

"Should we invite—" My voice trailed off, and I pointed in the direction of the newsroom where two or three visiting journalists were working.

"Why not?" Tammy said. "Let's ask Kevin and Walt and anyone who wants to come. The more the merrier."

"Let me clear it with Chris, and you all come up with plans. I need to do paperwork and I'll handle the online updates."

As they left, I moaned softly before I called Chris. Everything seemed like too much. I never finished one thing until I had something else to do.

"It's hard to let Tom go, isn't it?" Iris said from the door.

"Harder than I would have believed," I said. "He was part of my daily life."

"We're blessed in so many ways by the different people in our lives," she said. "Tom was the conscience of this paper for more than four decades."

"We've lost so much," I said. "Besides the tornado, there was my friend Ed, Aunt Helen and your Matt, and Chris lost Fran and—"

"Don't go there, Lois," Iris said quietly. "Think instead of the good, of how many people were spared, of your life in Green, your wonderful new husband."

"I'm thankful, but I think of Tom trying to save

us, driving out to the church with that wind blowing him all over the place. If it weren't for me, maybe he would be alive."

"Lois, if it weren't for your wedding, how many other people might have died? I might have been in my house when that tree crashed through the roof or the Craigs might have been home when their house split in two. We can't know. We don't have to know."

Choked up, I picked up the office phone which rang endlessly since it had been repaired.

"I didn't know, Lois, oh, I just heard," a crying voice said on the other end. "Are you OK? Is Chris OK?"

It was Marti.

"We're making it," I said, "but it's been a very rough week."

"I can't believe I didn't know," she wailed. "We landed in New York a few minutes ago on our way back to Ohio. I saw the story on Mannix on a news show in the airport."

"Calm down, and I'll tell you all about it," I said. "It started at the wedding."

I met Chris at the house site before the other guests arrived, and he had another surprise for me—a porch swing on a stand, sitting in what used to be the front yard.

"Stan picked it up in Shreveport when he went up for supplies," he said with a smile. "You told

146

me one time you never wanted to live anywhere again without a porch swing."

"We had some of our best moments in my old porch swing." I sat in the new swing. "I never knew it could be like this."

"Like what, sweetheart?"

"When I sit and visit with you, the cares of the world shrink."

"I feel the same way," Chris said.

We talked in the swing while the dogs played in the grass, as though they were happy to be home. Mannix was healing but clumsy and came to rest by us within a few minutes. Holly Beth, who had become his shadow, stayed close.

"Have you noticed anything different about Mannix?" Chris asked.

"You mean other than his big head because of all the attention he gets?"

"He doesn't bark anymore. He hasn't barked one time since he found Mr. Sepulvado. It's almost like after all that effort, he doesn't have anything to say."

I leaned over to pet Mannix. "You have the right to remain silent, sweet boy," I said.

"I sure am glad I married you," Chris said, draping his arm across the back of the swing.

"That was a great trip we had to Montana, wasn't it?" I asked.

"Hardly feels like we left at all. Have you thought anymore about where you want to live, Lois?"

147

"I'm not sure. When the dust settles, I guess we'll know. Right now we'd better get ready for our first party as a married couple—a funeral at our nonexistent house."

We set up two folding tables Chris had scrounged from his brothers and watched our guests pile out of pickups, SUVs, and cars, hauling covered dishes and lawn chairs. They looked more like they were going to a softball game than a memorial service. Gina, with a group of out-of-town journalists, arrived and mingled as though they had been part of the group forever, occasionally frowning as they swatted at mosquitoes. The smell of insect repellent hung in the air.

On a small plastic table borrowed from Pastor Jean, I made a display of a few of Tom's favorite things from his desk—a dog-eared dictionary, the copy of the newspaper with Katy's first byline, his green eyeshade, and an old picture-sizer that hadn't been used in years.

Iris Jo and Stan arrived together and stood hand in hand by the table, placing a Bible nearby, open to the Twenty-third Psalm. Katy read the passage aloud, her voice breaking when she came to the part about walking through the valley of the shadow of death.

Looking at the group assembled under the trees, she held up the Bible and swallowed hard. "I learned from Pastor Jean that life's easier when it's shared. She taught me that a rope is stronger

148

when woven with multiple strands. I'm happy Tom was woven into my life, all of our lives, and that we can support one another."

She laid the Bible back on the table and hurried over to Molly. Her words soothed my ragged edges. "Katy may join you in the pulpit one of these days," I said to Jean. "She may turn out not to be a journalist after all."

As the night progressed, friends joked and told affectionate stories about Tom, such as the time he drove off from a gas pump with the hose still in his car, his editorial crusade against people who didn't use their blinkers, and how he planned his social outings around the due dates of library books.

"Remember when he got that black eye playing putt-putt? He blamed it on the windmill hole," Alex said. "Claimed the ball hit the blade and flew back at him."

"He pretended like he hated TV," Katy said, "but he watched *Frasier* reruns every night."

"And *King of the Hill*," Molly said. "He loved that show, even though he didn't seem like a cartoon kind of guy."

"Remember when I told him I was planning an 'apple and pewter' wedding?" Tammy asked. "I believe his exact words were, 'Would those be the colors formerly known as red and gray?'"

Individuals gathered, visiting, laughing and crying, feeling the copy editor's presence all around us. Kevin walked up behind me as I stood looking at the items from Tom's desk. She had arrived a few minutes earlier with Asa, who was playing a gleeful game of chase with Molly and Katy.

"He was special to you, wasn't he?" she asked.

"Yes," I said, and leaned against her shoulder. "Have you noticed how people come in and out of our lives, and we're never quite the same again?"

"Every life counts," Kevin said. "People live in many different ways and they touch us along the way."

"Speaking of special people, where's Terrence tonight?"

She pulled back slightly. "Terrence?"

"You know. Tall, handsome, attorney from Alexandria. Drives a fancy car. Brought you to my wedding a week ago."

"I doubt we'll see much more of him," she said.

I twisted my head and knew my face had a weird quizzical look. "Did he get a big case?"

"I'm not going to date him after all," Kevin said.

"I thought you were crazy about him."

"He's a fantastic man," she said, "but I can't put Asa through that."

"Through what?"

"Little A.C. lost his mother and sisters in that fire and then Papa Levi in the tornado. I can't risk letting him get close and then Terrence going away or us breaking up. It would break his heart."

"Are you thinking of Asa's heart or your own?"

"It's been a brutal week, Lois," Kevin said. "I can't talk about this right now."

"I know you've seen things this week that I can't even imagine, but don't give up on men because of it."

"I won't."

"He might not break your heart."

"He could."

"Sometimes hearts don't get broken. I'm living proof that there's someone for everyone."

"You can say that again," she said. "I'd better rescue those girls from my son and head back to the hospital."

I moseyed to the rear of the yard and kicked around in the late evening light, looking for a trace of anything left by the tornado. Spring night noises, eerie sounds of loud frogs and insects, alternated between making me happy and scaring me. I found nothing, except for the occasional shard of unrecognizable glass or twisted piece of metal.

Gina wandered up with a Diet Dr Pepper and a homemade brownie Chris's mom had sent. "This is the best food I've ever tasted," she said. "Do people down here eat like this all the time?"

"All the time," I said. "Even better much of the time."

"If Zach doesn't send me home soon, I'll have to order new clothes."

"You could borrow some of mine," I said, "but I seem to be missing a few items."

"This is a beautiful spot," she said, with the look everyone got when they stared at the spot where the house had been. "You lived out here?"

"For two years," I said. "It was a charming old cottage. The screened porch was there," I pointed. "The kitchen window was over here. It's hard to think that I stood at that window only a week ago."

"Will you and Chris build another house here?"

"I'm not sure. We haven't been up to discussing it in any detail. I suppose we'll either build here or buy a house on Bayou Lake."

"I've driven around the lake," she said. "It's posh. But this place is so secluded, special somehow. Your yard must have been spectacular."

"Old plants are the best," I said, "and I hope they survive. Most of those were planted by Helen McCuller, the woman who gave me this house."

"Someone gave you a house?"

"Sounds crazy, doesn't it? It started as a loaner, complete with rats, but when I decided to keep the newspaper, the house was a gift."

"I admire you, Lois," Gina said. "You did what most people only talk about. You broke away from the corporate world and made a whole new life."

"This was the right move for me, but it wouldn't be for everyone," I said. "Green has convinced me, though, that there is a right place for every single person."

We strolled as we talked, daylight nearly past. I

152

kicked a sweet-gum ball, and Gina looked down and reached under a bush, pulling out a small book. It was my journal, the ink smeared and pages swollen. I flipped it open and found the delicate pink dogwood bloom.

"I put this in here the morning of my wedding," I said. "What in the world kept it from flying away with the tornado?"

"Maybe it was right where it was supposed to be," Gina said.

11

Rachel Winn says this is the last call to claim the patio furniture that blew into her yard during the storm. "I've got the pinkeye and have to go to Shreveport to the eye doctor," she said. "If no one calls by tomorrow evening, I'll put it out by the street and let whoever wants it take it."
—The Green News-Item

Iris Jo walked into my office mid-morning on Monday, dressed in a beautiful new outfit.

"Are you and Chris free for lunch?" she asked.

"Chris had to report to work," I said. "They're assessing the school and deciding when to reopen. I'll be around, though."

"I hoped you both could come," she said, a slight frown on her face.

153

"Want to plan for another day?"

"I've got my heart set on today."

"Where do you want to go?"

"The park by the lake," she said, mentioning the place we often walked during lunch.

"The park? Aren't you a little overdressed for that?"

"Stan and I are getting married at noon," she said with a big smile. "We want you and Chris to be our witnesses."

"You're getting married?" My voice came out in a croak. "Today? At lunch?"

Iris laughed loudly, a bold sound I'd never heard from her before.

"I said I'd never marry again after Matt's father ran off," she said. "But that's been such a long time ago. I've prayed about it and know this is right. I don't want to wait another day to get married. No offense to my neighbors at the Lakeside Motel, but I'm ready to move in with Stan. My house won't be repaired for months."

I took both of her hands in mine. "I'm not sure how to say this, but you're not rushing into this because of the tornado, are you? Things are stressful, but they'll settle down."

"Oh, my," she said.

"What?"

"It's a scary day when you're the one trying to calm me down," she said. "I'll admit the storm reminded me how unpredictable life can be. I've

154

known for months, maybe years, I wanted to marry Stan. I've wasted enough time."

"He's a good man," I said. "As an old married lady, I can tell you that you're going to be extremely happy together."

"Do you like my outfit?" She did a little twirl, and the skirt spun with her. "Your seamstress Barbara made it for me, in one day. She said she needed a project to make her feel good after the storm." The dress was a simple purple shift, the color of a beautiful purple Louisiana iris, with a matching jacket.

"I thought you were mighty dressed up for a work day," I said. "It's beautiful, and the color is perfect."

"That was Stan's request." She sounded almost shy. "He says I'm prettier than a field full of irises. Isn't that the sweetest thing?"

I rushed at her for a big hug. She hugged me back, but almost at arm's length.

"Watch my port," she said with a smile, pointing underneath the dress where she got her chemo treatment. I eased my grip, a moment of sadness marring my joy.

"Shouldn't you have taken the day off?" I asked.

"I've missed way too much work since my surgery," she said, "and we've wasted enough time."

"That's the truth," Stan said, walking into my office, wearing his usual pressman's uniform,

155

including a hat made out of folded newsprint. "I've been trying to get Iris Jo to marry me for years. They say every cloud has a silver lining, and this is certainly mine."

"I'd better try to track Chris down," I said. "Have you told Tammy and the others?"

"Everyone's running around like chickens with their heads chopped off," Iris said, "and we don't want to make a fuss. Linda's over at the courthouse, and Tammy dashed in and out, said she was covering a story with Katy."

"But this is a big deal," I said.

"Pastor Jean will be there to say a few words and give us her blessing," Iris said. "I'll miss the girls, but getting married to this man is wedding enough for me. I don't want to complicate things for everyone else."

She looked radiant in the purple dress. She had a scarf around her hair, which was falling out in clumps.

"Stan, are you at least going to change clothes?" I asked with a grin. "Maybe lose the hat?"

I hurried down the street to the florist and burst in on Becca and her helper, piecing together a funeral spray out of silk flowers. Two or three other arrangements set nearby, white gladiolus and carnations in a container with a fan-shaped handle and a basket of mums that looked as though they had been spray painted pastel pink and blue.

"Know anything about flower arranging?" Becca asked. "We finally got a shipment of flowers in and we're overwhelmed."

"My mother had a green thumb," I said, "but I didn't inherit it."

I glanced around at the plastic buckets of containers filled with fresh flowers and a cabinet loaded with silk flowers of every variety. A few blooming kalanchoes in baskets sat on a table, and the floor was lined with rubber trees and peace lilies, plants that made me think of my mom's funeral.

"More services?" I asked.

"One today and another tomorrow," Becca said, shaking her head. "I may be the only person in town whose business was helped by the storm. It's been a grueling week. Decorating Grace Chapel for your wedding was the last fun thing I did."

"The church looked the way I always imagined—before the roof caved in," I said. "You are so creative."

Becca lived in the small Ashland community and had opened the flower and gift business a little more than a year ago in a run-down storefront, but I had not gotten to know her well. She had a head for business and was well thought of around town.

"Are you here to follow up on the Green Forward meeting, or do you need flowers?" she asked.

"I hope you can help with another fun order," I

said, my eyes scanning the counter and lifting the bucket I needed. "I know you're swamped, but could you put together a simple bouquet of these tied with a ribbon?"

A strange look passed over her face. "Like a bride's bouquet?" she asked.

"Exactly," I said. "Nothing fancy but it has to be those purple irises."

"Must be a trend," she said. "Can you pick them up this afternoon?"

"I know I'm asking a lot, but I need them now. They're for a friend."

"Let me guess," she said. "Gotta have them by noon."

I ran by the Lakeside Motel and shook the wrinkles out of the one special occasion dress I had packed for our honeymoon. I had planned to wear it out to dinner one evening at the lodge and hadn't bothered taking it out of the suitcase when we checked in. I didn't figure I'd need to dress up anytime soon.

Even though the motel was close to the park, I had to detour around the Lakeside neighborhood, avoiding repairmen whose truck logos suggested they worked on electrical lines, telephones, and cable television. The pervasive damage in the old neighborhood contrasted with the beauty of the day, blue tarps on roofs, trees uprooted, and gutters sagging.

Chris met me at the park, wearing jeans and my favorite of his knit shirts, the one he'd worn the night he asked me to date him. "You look so pretty," he said. "I'm sorry I didn't have time to change."

"I'm happy you were able to slip away," I said. "Everything OK at school?"

"We're getting pressure from the state to get classes started back this week," he said. "We're not even sure how we'll get buses down many of the roads yet."

Pastor Jean arrived next, followed closely by Iris and Stan, whose usual serious face looked almost giddy. He had changed into creased jeans and a starched shirt and kept his hand on Iris Jo's elbow, as though guiding her toward the altar.

"That man is protective of his bride," Jean said, as he ushered Iris to the path by the lake. I produced the bouquet of irises from behind my back and handed them to Iris, whose smile got even more beautiful.

"Oh, Lois, they're perfect," she said.

Jean, wearing what I knew to be her favorite blue dress, pulled out her Bible and arranged us as though we stood in front of a full house in a cathedral, assuming the solemn and rich voice I loved so much.

"Friends," she said with a smile, "we've gathered today to—"

"Photographer's here," Tammy yelled as she

pulled into the parking lot. "Don't start without us."

She and Linda practically ran down to where we were, Linda holding a bouquet of purple irises. "For you," she said to Iris, and then laughed when she saw the flowers in the bride's hand.

"You didn't actually think you could keep this from us, did you?" Tammy asked, snapping pictures while she talked.

"I should have known better," Iris Jo said, while Stan looked bemused.

"Clerk of court records," Linda said. "I saw where you got a marriage license last week. I just wasn't sure when you'd use it."

"That dress was a dead giveaway," Tammy said. "We ruled out Grace Community Chapel, since it's a mess, and you weren't at the courthouse. This was our last guess."

Pastor Jean cleared her throat and started over. "Friends, this is a special—"

"Wait for us," Katy's voice called, and I looked up to see her and Molly running full out through the park, Katy carrying a bundle of irises wrapped in green tissue.

"I thought you said the courthouse," Katy said to Tammy. Panting, she handed the bouquet to Iris Jo with a look of disappointment. "I didn't think anyone else would think of these."

"They're beautiful," Iris said, nestling the three bouquets in her arms.

"Might this be a good time to continue?" Jean asked.

"For the love of heaven, yes," Stan, the most patient man I had ever met, said.

Iris smiled and put her arm around his waist.

"Beloved friends," Jean said, "this is a joyful day, when love triumphs."

Chris reached for my hand.

"We gather here, in a spot that reminds us of the beauty of life, to join this couple in marriage."

The world stopped for the next few minutes. The solemnity of the ceremony matched any I had attended, and a thread of jubilation was woven through it. Birds sang, and the first hints of wisteria climbed through trees, so fragrant it made me want to gulp its scent. Iris and Stan stared into each other's eyes. My handsome husband stood near.

Stan winked at Iris, and tears welled in my eyes.

"Now the formal photographs," Tammy said.

"Formal?" Chris whispered.

"Humor her," I said, and lined up with the bride and groom, Katy and Molly, all the women, the two men, every combination you could imagine.

"Enough," Chris said. "Stan, give me a hand, will you?"

The two walked to Chris's truck, my husband slapping the new groom on the back and then shaking his hand. They returned from the parking lot with two stacks of box lunches from the Cotton Boll Café.

"The wedding lunch," Chris said. "It's amazing what you can come up with if you're willing to beg."

"Just married" was written on each box, with large hand-drawn red hearts. Even in the midst of chaos, the grill staff took time for the small gesture, one of the touches that made Green the place it was.

"I ordered extras to deliver to a few other folks," Chris said. "We have plenty for the wedding crashers."

Under the trees, we ate turkey sandwiches and homemade pie and laughed and talked.

"So you're going to live at Stan's?" Linda asked.

"For now," Iris said.

"I won't be able to keep her away from Route Two for long," Stan said.

"This super handyman here is going to build us a new house when things settle down," Iris said. "I'm finally going to have a den that didn't used to be a place to park cars."

"And I'm going to have a pool table," Stan said.

I threw Chris a look. "Don't start getting ideas," I said.

"Miss Iris Jo, did you two start dating while I was in New York last summer?" Katy asked. "I never even knew you liked each other . . . in that way." She hemmed and hawed. "I didn't know you were in love."

Katy's magazine internship had taken her away from Green for only a few months, but, with the ego of a near eighteen-year-old, she still seemed to be afraid she had missed something. She had dated Iris Jo's son, Matt, who had been killed in a car wreck nearly three years ago, and she clung to Iris at times.

"I'd been trying to get this woman to go out on a date with me for five or six years," Stan, usually a man of few words, said. "She held out on me until Lois convinced her."

"Me?" I asked. "I thought you were an item when I got here."

"An item at the *Item*," Molly said with a laugh. "I like that."

"I didn't realize it for a while, but I got brave when I saw Lois falling for Chris," Iris said, her fingers linked through her new husband's. "I figured if she'd take a chance on love I would too."

"Here's to Lois," Stan said, raising his plastic cup of tea.

"And to the newest newlyweds," Pastor Jean said. "At this rate, I can marry the entire town off within a matter of weeks."

With pollen sifting down in a cloud of yellow, the conversation was relaxed and happy. I not only relished the marriage, but the simple blessing of sitting in the park together.

Tornadoes, cancer, and funerals were, for a time, powerless.

The joy of the wedding thawed a piece of my heart that had been frozen for the past nine days.

Reluctant to return to phone calls and insurance claims and crisis after crisis, I dawdled while the others packed up. Chris and I stood in the parking lot and watched them leaving.

"That may have been the best wedding I've ever been to," I said.

"Aren't you forgetting one?"

"OK, second best wedding," I said. "Life almost felt right. Will things ever get back to normal?"

"Define 'normal,'" Chris said. "As I recall, our lives have never been exactly normal."

"We didn't realize how good we had it. I want to run home and get under the bed, except I don't have a home to run to."

Chris sat the boxes of leftovers on the hood of his truck and turned to me. "Come here," he said, and drew me into his arms with a tenderness that brought tears to my eyes.

"Between covering the story and living right in the middle of it, I haven't had time to think. Coming out here today—" Tears began to flow, and I couldn't stop them.

Chris grabbed a wad of napkins out of his truck,

and I wiped my face furiously. I had never had a meltdown like this in front of Chris, and I felt slightly embarrassed.

"I'm such a baby," I said. "We're much better off than most people."

"Lois, you don't have to hold the entire town together. You're entitled to a few tears now and then . . . or even a lot of tears. Everyone in Green has probably shed plenty in the past week."

"What are we going to do about a house, and how can the *Item* keep up with everything?"

"You'll figure out the newspaper challenges," he said. "Your brain is only one of the many things I love about you. The rest of it we'll handle together. We'll get used to a new routine and take care of a few things we didn't count on."

"A few dozen things. Right when life was supposed to settle down, it imploded. Everything I had blew away."

My husband cupped my face in his big, calloused hands and looked deep into my eyes. "I'm still here."

12

*The senior class of Green High has
moved its prom to the Bayou Lake pavilion,
and faculty sponsors are requesting more
chaperones. If they don't get enough,
they'll have to hire security from the parish,
which will cut into the refreshment budget.
Rumor has it that they are going to have a
chocolate fountain this year. If you would like
to help, please call the school office.*
                    —*The Green News-Item*

A producer from New York called on the Thursday before Easter, in the midst of a newsroom argument about whether we'd gone overboard with tornado coverage.

"People need a dose of good news," Tammy said. "We should cover the Lakeside Association Easter egg hunt and get pictures of the azaleas blooming in front of the library."

"It's only been a month," Alex said. "We've barely scratched the surface on construction permits and the long-term impact. This place is going to dry up and blow away."

"Don't you think you're being a little dramatic, Alex? Green made it through the Great Depression, boll weevils, and tuberculosis. I doubt a tornado will be the end of it." Linda, on deadline with a story for Friday's edition, didn't look up as she shuffled through her notes and jumped into the discussion.

"I wonder what Tom would have thought?" Katy asked, and the room got quiet.

When the phone rang, no one moved to pick it up.

After five rings, I snatched the receiver off the phone on the composing room wall. "Hello," I barked, sounding like I expected a telemarketer on the other end.

"Excuse me," a man with a distinct East Coast accent said. "I'm trying to reach *The Green News-Item*."

"This is the *Item*."

"Lois Barker Craig, please," the man said in a tone that sounded far more like a demand than a request.

"This is Lois."

"I need to speak to the owner of the newspaper," he said.

"You're speaking to her."

"I see," he said, and there was the clicking of computer keys in the background.

"May I help you?" I asked.

"I'm calling to help you," he said. "My network intends to feature you on our Sunday evening program."

"I beg your pardon?"

"To mark the one-month anniversary of the

tornado, we're doing a story on Green, Louisiana." The name of the town sounded odd from his mouth. "We will record the footage Sunday morning and broadcast to millions that evening in a special report."

"I'm afraid there's no room in the parking lot for your equipment," I said, "but you're welcome to use our newsroom." A steady stream of journalists had passed through over the past four weeks. While the staff had adapted, readers complained loudly about the lack of customer parking.

"We don't want parking, Ms. Craig," the man said. "We want you."

"I understand," I said, although I didn't at all.

"Our researchers told us about the phenomenal coverage your newspaper has pulled off and the leadership role you've taken in the community."

"Zach put you up to this, didn't he?" I asked. "Gina said he was still ticked at me for leaving Dayton and the company. Tell him my newspaper is twice the paper his was, and—"

"Ms. Craig," the producer interrupted, "this is no prank. We want you to tell the country about how your little town has fought back."

"It's not my little town," I said. "Everyone has stepped in to help. Perhaps you might give Mayor Eva Hillburn a call."

"We'll certainly talk to the mayor," he said. "But we want to tell the story of a courageous journalist who rushed to the newspaper in her wedding gown to cover the big story."

I gasped. Every eye in the newsroom was glued to me, and I could tell they were trying to figure out who I was talking to. "Are you kidding me?"

"You're a hero," he said.

"You make this sound like a soap opera. Real people's lives were affected. People died."

"We'll explain all of that in the program, of course."

"You clearly did not see my interview the morning after the tornado," I said, "or you would not ask me to appear on television. This Sunday won't be possible. It's Easter, and I intend to be at church with my husband and friends."

"Perhaps our crews could accompany you."

"To worship services?" I asked. "These people need privacy and time to heal. They don't need one more news crew in their faces."

"That attitude does not fit with the aggressive coverage your newspaper has done on the storm, including scooping the national media in virtually every angle of this story for the past four weeks."

"We're the local newspaper," I said, my voice rising. "We help people find answers to their questions and solutions to their problems."

"An excellent way to phrase that," he said, as though I had won a middle-school oration competition. "This will add national exposure to your work and draw attention to the plight of your people."

"The plight of my people? I'm not a dictator in a Third World country. I must get back to work."

"What they say is true then," he said.

"What who say?"

"The national media are buzzing about the feisty owner of a twice-weekly paper in a Podunk town in Louisiana. They say you get phenomenal work out of a staff that is smaller than our secretarial pool."

I faltered. *The national media were buzzing about me?*

"My tiny staff is preparing a forty-eight-page special edition for tomorrow, with Pulitzer-Prize worthy photos and narratives that will make you cry," I said. "I must go."

"Our program can bring these stories alive in ways that a newspaper can't," he said. "At least take my name and number."

I jotted the information and hung up.

"Podunk," I said. "A hotshot big shot in New York says Green is a Podunk town."

"Didn't you say that, too, when you moved here?" Tammy asked.

"I never once used the word *Podunk*," I said. "Except maybe to my friend Marti."

"So what was that all about?" Linda asked.

"A superstar network reporter wants to come

170

down and shadow me on Sunday, let me do a dog and pony show about Green."

"That's awesome," Katy said, jumping up. "Can I be on camera?"

"I wouldn't do that in a million years," I said. "We're friends and neighbors to these people. I'm not going to make a spectacle out of them."

"Would it rally support?" Linda asked. "Could this program raise money and bring in extra volunteers? Local people are fading fast."

"Lois, the national coverage has been hit-and-run," Alex said, an excited expression on his face. "This might bring the story back to the forefront."

"I'll be there in time for the sermon," I told Chris Sunday morning. "It'll be crowded, so save me a seat."

"Are you sure this is a good idea?" he asked. "With folding chairs in the parking lot, everything's going to be out of whack. It's going to be hard enough on everyone as it is."

"Pastor Jean said it might help gain attention for aid dollars," I said, "and mission volunteers from around the country. The poor are homeless. They can't afford a hotel room like we've got, and you've seen firsthand how much help we need with meals."

"I'm certainly not going to argue with both you and Jean," Chris said. "I'll see you at church."

I made my way downtown, continually shocked

171

at the destruction. Tom's car had finally been towed, and my breath caught in my throat when I passed the site. "I hope I'm doing the right thing, friend," I whispered.

The television crew, complete with megastar reporter Drew Durrett, had set up on the steps of the *Item* by the time I pulled up. Unlike what I had always heard about TV announcers, he was as tall and striking in person as on the screen, although I suspected he colored his hair. He wore tailored slacks and a pink linen shirt without a wrinkle in it, an outfit most men in Green wouldn't be caught dead in.

"We'll interview you, get a few shots around town, and wrap up at your church service," he said. "We'll catch you live right before it airs this evening, the most watched news program on television."

My staff had prepped me for the appearance, throwing hard questions at me about economic impact and emergency preparedness. Drew's first questions were how it felt to spend my wedding night at the newspaper and was it true that my husband had given his home away only days before mine blew away.

Then he wanted to know if I found it ironic that an odd weather system from the Midwest had caused the unusual storm.

"A bizarre coincidence," I said after a couple of seconds of opening my mouth with no sound coming out. "My story is one of hundreds in our community. The town of Green and Bouef Parish ask for the compassion and prayers of the country."

Katy, who had insisted on being on hand, gave me a thumbs-up sign.

"While this story may be old news for viewers," I said, "it continues to unfold in very real ways for individuals here. The statistics are not merely numbers but heartache and financial ruin. As the local newspaper, *The Green News-Item* will follow this story as long as needed."

"Nice job in taking back the interview," Katy whispered as we rode out to Grace Chapel. "You were awesome."

"It's clear you care about this town," Drew said, obviously having heard Katy's every word. "Your passion is impressive."

As we drove up to the edge of the church site, I wanted to crawl under the seat of the car. Every person in the church turned, and some waved. *What had I been thinking?*

"We're later than I anticipated," I said in a low voice to the reporter. "Perhaps we could wait over here until after the service."

"The Easter celebration is a major part of the story," Drew said. "Wc want to show the resilience of people in the midst of a storm. You've told me that faith is a key component of their lives."

I looked across the parking lot to where the damaged church sat. Someone had hung beautiful sprays of lilies on the front doors. Familiar blue tarps covered the missing roof, and the piano, only slightly damaged, had been moved outside for the service.

Every seat was filled with friends and neighbors, many dressed in their Easter best, and a few people stood at the ends of aisles. The sun shone bright but the air was cool, a typical Easter morning in North Louisiana.

"I'll meet you here after the service," I said to Drew and the camera crew. While Katy slipped in next to her mother and stepfather, I walked quickly to the empty plastic folding seat next to Chris. I met Pastor Jean's eyes, and she gave the tiniest of nods but never missed a word.

"'Do not be afraid,' the angels told the shepherds on the night Christ was born," Jean said. "'Do not be afraid,' they said when the women found an empty tomb. 'Do not be afraid,' they tell us here today on this day that reminds us we can always go on."

"Amen," an older church member said.

"Amen," Iris Jo said.

"And amen again," said a voice it took me a minute to place. It was Hugh, my father-in-law.

Pianist Mary Frances pounded out a medley of traditional Easter hymns, making the small instrument with water spots sound as beautiful as a baby grand. The crowd listened prayerfully, many with heads bowed, others with tears flowing.

"Go in peace," Jean said as we rose for the benediction, "but don't go too far because we'll eat dinner on the grounds in about twenty minutes."

Tables of food were pulled out of Jean's parsonage, and the worship chairs became dining chairs. I was patted and praised and encouraged by everyone, from Estelle, who reported that Holly Beth missed me, to Iris, who suggested we might get new advertisers from the broadcast.

Drew interviewed Jean inside the sodden church, standing cautiously in front of the altar where Chris and I had been married. I trailed along. The beautiful quilted banner was stained and probably ruined. A piece of ceiling tile hung by a corner.

"It was miraculous," Jean said, pulling Drew by the arm through the safe parts of the church. "Because so many people were here for the wedding, they were not harmed. Trees fell on their houses, and if they'd been on the roads, they might have been killed."

When we stepped outside, Maria walked up with her three boys and looked at the popular newsman. "I must tell this reporter my story," she said in careful English, her voice shaking. "I would have no story were it not for Chris and Lois Craig. They gave me that home there."

She pointed across the road.

"My sons and I lived in a rented shack, and it blew away. We would be dead if not for these two." As she spoke, her voice became clear and strong, her Spanish accent making her words sound like a song. "Lois and Chris gave us a true home in Green, not merely a place to live but a chance to be part of their family."

"Thank you for those heartfelt words," Drew said to Maria, shaking her hand. "You have beautiful sons."

"They saved an unconscious man covered in fire ants," Katy said, moving close to the reporter. "He was nearly dead." As the camera zoomed in, she chatted with the reporter as though she were on national television every day. While I felt stiff and clammy, she was a natural.

I could see Drew's eyes brighten as he turned back to me. "What a delightful young woman," he said, "with a flair for human interest. Lois, you never mentioned these stories."

"They're exaggerating," I said, frowning at Katy. "Could I interest you in lunch? You won't get food like this in New York City." I sounded the city's name as though I were on a game show.

By the middle of the afternoon, I felt tireder than I had the morning after the tornado and more anxious than when a series of fires had been set at the paper by the now dead Chuck McCuller, big-time jerk.

"If you would gather your staff and friends at our van at five o'clock your time, we'll introduce you live and move into the recorded segment," Drew said, after eating what I was fairly certain were two large plates of ham and potato salad and three desserts. Nearly every person at Grace Chapel had moseyed by, to be hospitable or smoothed their hair and walked right in front of the cameras.

As we gathered for the broadcast that afternoon, Drew's motor home was parked on the street by the paper, and the crowd was larger than attendance at my wedding, gradually building until it looked like Green's summer ice cream festival. A giant monitor sat to the side, and people waved at the cameras as though outside a Manhattan studio for a morning show.

Someone had written "Welcome to Green: Home of the Green High Rabbits" on a poster, complete with the school mascot drawn with green paint. The youth minister from the Baptist church down the street held a sign that said, "He is Risen."

My stomach felt like I had eaten too much of Estelle's banana pudding and one too many of Pastor Jean's legendary deviled eggs.

"How's it going?" Kevin whispered in my ear, and I almost squealed with happiness.

"I've never been so happy to see anyone in my

177

life. Help! What do you recommend for an upset stomach?"

"That rough?" As usual, she looked gorgeous, her dark hair swept up, the slight smell of Dove soap on her skin. She wore a pair of yellow jeans that would have made me feel like a float in a parade, but looked like an advertisement in a spring catalog on her.

"Where's Asa Corinthian?" I scanned the crowd.

"Over there with Mama and Daddy," she said. "They wouldn't have missed this for the world." Marcus and Pearl sat on the edge of the crowd in lawn chairs. Asa, dressed in his Easter suit, was playing peekaboo with Molly, who wore a giant smile.

"Are you having déjà vu?" Kevin asked. "Doesn't this remind you of the crowd at the first newspaper fire on New Year's Day last year?"

"Isn't it something?"

"It's wonderful. It's the first time I've seen most of these people smile in a month."

"I've hardly seen you," I said. "The doctoring clearly isn't slowing down."

"Not much." She shook her head. "We're getting more of the stress-related ailments now. As the shock wears off, people's emotions are coming out in headaches and high blood pressure. By the time I make rounds after clinic, I barely see my son."

"Are you OK?" I put my hand on her arm. As I looked closer I could see the strain of fatigue on her face.

"It feels unreal that Papa Levi's dead. Every day I think he'll be sitting with A.C. when I get home. I miss him so much, more than I expected."

"I feel the same way about Tom," I said, digging in my pocket for a Kleenex. "I relied on his opinion much more than I realized."

A loud giggle from Asa caught our attention, and I turned to see him on Chris's shoulders headed our way.

"Isn't he adorable?" Kevin asked.

"Your son or my husband?"

"Both. You're a great friend, Lois. Happy Easter."

"Lois, that reporter guy's looking for you," Chris said. "It's about time to start."

"Say a prayer," I said, giving Asa and Chris a quick peck on the cheek.

I squirmed throughout the broadcast, groaning out loud when I saw—and heard—myself on camera.

"Do I really sound like that?" I whispered to Chris.

"My southern bride. I believe you've picked up an accent."

I moaned when the reporter described me as a kind of paragon of community journalism and glowed when he talked about my "fine" staff. I

179

beamed at how friendly and smart Katy sounded. The crowd hooted and pointed when their neighbors were interviewed, and overall the story had an affectionate tone.

"This is Drew Durrett, signing off from Green, Louisiana, where the people are hard-working and God-fearing . . . and will never give up hope." The crowd milled around, slow to leave.

Pastor Jean pulled Maria's sons in their big red wagon to where I stood. "I love to watch how God uses you," she said.

"What in the world are you talking about now, Pastor?" I smiled at the three boys as we spoke.

"The ancient words of the resurrection and a live television broadcast. Only Lois Barker Craig could bring those two together with such ease."

"Ease?" I said with a snort. "My deodorant quit working hours ago."

Jean laughed. "Easy or not, you stepped up to use your unique gifts right when they were most needed."

Nearly everyone I'd ever met in Green came by to say thanks, ranging from Rose, whose antique mall had been squarely behind the live shots, and Anna Grace, leaning against her walker, Bud next to her. I didn't tell them I had tried to weasel out of the interview.

The crowd shifted slightly, and a path opened to show Mayor Eva making her way toward me, looking like royalty in a silk suit and matching heels. She took both my hands and pulled me to her.

"We turned a corner today, thanks to you," she said. "You showed the glory of Green."

13

*Summer Montgomery of the Ringgold
community had an excellent performance
at T-ball this week, according to her
Mamaw Evelyn. "She found seven four-leaf
clovers during one game," Evelyn said.
"Things like that do not happen
every day, and we think that newspaper
photographer should have come out
here to get a picture." This correspondent
reminds you we welcome reader snapshots
as long as they are not too blurry.*
—The Green News-Item

Katy and Molly wore gardenias on their graduation gowns, a Green High tradition.

The smell of the luscious white flowers and the sight of the girls as they prepared to line up outside the high school gym made my heart nearly pop.

Both were headed to well-regarded southern universities with intense admissions requirements.

"Aren't they amazing?" I asked Tammy, who, as usual, was snapping photos.

"Totally amazing," she said. "Stand over here so I can get the three of you together."

Chris and other teachers stood on the stage to give out diplomas to the fifty-three members of the class, shaking hands with sheepish boys and hugging the girls, most of whom they had watched grow up.

Katy's stepfather, the superintendent of schools, said a few words and stepped in to present Katy's diploma, a move that seemed to catch her off guard. As her mother stood from the side to snap a photograph, Katy put her arms around her stepfather, her forehead on his chest for a second. "I love you," she whispered, the words picked up by the cordless microphone attached to his lapel.

I wept.

"Katy had such a tough time accepting him," I whispered with a sniff as the stream of graduates continued across the stage. "He never gave up on her. I'm so proud of that young woman."

Iris laughed softly. "You sound like her mother."

"I'm old enough to be her mother."

After the students crossed the wide stage, the principal announced their plans. For Katy, he said, "University of Georgia, broadcast journalism."

My heart jumped up into my throat, and my eyes met Katy's.

"Sorry, Lois," she mouthed and then waved her diploma in the air and smiled as the audience clapped.

"Broadcast?" My voice was way too loud.

"Shhh," a woman behind me said.

I looked at Iris. "Did you know?"

"She told me a couple of weeks ago. The taste of television on Easter got her attention."

"Shhh," the person said again, and I sat up straighter and shut up, my mind whirling with shock. I had fantasized about Katy moving back to Green after college and taking over the *Item* one day. A broadcast degree probably meant she intended to do neither.

When Molly's name was called, her mother and brothers and sisters stood and cheered, and she smiled shyly and blew them a kiss as she started across the stage.

"University of Florida, business administration," the principal announced.

I clapped so hard my hands hurt, and I heard one of Tammy's loud whistles. We had worked hard to get Molly's business scholarship to Florida, pulling old newspaper strings. We spent hours wrapping up application packets.

"Their essays will have to be top-notch," Katy's stepfather had said. "The big colleges don't have much respect for Green High. Not prestigious enough."

Knowing Molly was going to get a first-class education helped make up for Katy's secret change of heart. "Broadcast journalism?" I muttered to Iris. "Haven't I taught her anything?"

The aspiring TV journalist found me outside the main door of the school auditorium, the shade welcome on the early June morning.

"I'm sorry," Katy said. "I was going to tell you, but I was afraid you'd be mad."

"I am mad."

"I'll still be doing journalism."

"It's not the same. It's surface stuff."

"The stories about Green haven't been shallow," she said. "They've made a huge difference."

"Not all of them." I suspected I sounded like the teenager in this conversation.

She took the gardenia from her gown and fastened it to my dress, holding my shoulder when I tried to pull back.

"Don't be mad," she said. "You're my inspiration. I was headed to beauty school when I first met you. You knew I was a journalist before I did."

By the end of June it was clear that change was here to stay, and I might as well get used to it. My disappointment at Katy's career path had been replaced by my dismay about her and Molly leaving for college in a little more than a month. I figured out that Alex had interviewed with two regional newspapers. Chris was complaining about our need to find a new place to live.

I had also become a celebrity. I had been interviewed a half dozen more times by television stations, national magazines, and major newspapers, eager to show the spirit of small-town America and exploit the story of a former big-city journalist who had found happiness with a catfish farmer and a three-legged dog.

My friend Marti called from Dayton to say the newsroom was envious of my fame.

"You're a star. Every time I look up, you're on television. Yesterday Gary brought in a magazine and a newspaper with stories about the rebirth of Green and the lovely Lois Craig."

"You're full of it," I said. "You know how the media are. Where one reporter goes, they all go."

"Nice to see you haven't lost your respect for the profession."

I felt a blush crawling up my face. "It's nice and hot down here. Isn't it about time for your annual visit?"

"Sweet change of subject. I told you I'm not coming until you get out of that motel. I want to see your new place."

"Stay tuned. No news there yet."

"Maybe you could make the search into a reality show."

"I'd love to chat," I said, laughing, "but I have a photo shoot with a magazine."

"Seriously?"

"Walking in the door." I hung up and went to greet the guest.

The photo process was tedious, and I looked in

the mirror a dozen times to see if my hair was in place. As usual, the staff gathered around, either to give moral support or slip into one of the shots.

After the freelance photographer had dismantled her lighting and left the building, Molly paused from pasting up a page of classified advertising.

"You're a player," she said.

"I haven't played in so long I don't know what it feels like," I said, rubbing my neck.

"She means you're a mover and shaker," Tammy said. "You've got to admit it's sort of fun."

"Have you noticed she gets more attention from the television interviews?" Katy asked. "Everywhere I go people tell me they saw Miss Lois on the TV." She spoke the last sentence imitating the voice of the country members of Grace Community.

"I'm ignoring you. You'll come to your senses one of these days," I said.

"Who would have thought a tornado would make you famous?" Tammy said, fidgeting with her necklace of bright beads. "You're finally trendy."

"Who's famous?" Iris Jo asked, walking in from her office, a pink bandanna around her bald head.

"Our fearless leader," Katy said. "My stepdad says she's a media darling."

"I don't want to be a media darling."

"Sure you do," Tammy said. "Why else would you do it?"

"I'm not sure."

"To help the town?" Molly asked.

"To increase advertising?" Iris Jo asked. "Because if that's the case, I'm all for it. I'm working on the books for the second quarter, and we're taking on water. We've got to bring in more revenue."

"We'd better do it quick," Alex said, "because by the end of the summer, the national guys won't even know Green exists."

Holly Beth jumped down from the scratchy newsroom couch and ran over to Katy. The puppy came to work with me most of the time and had become the newspaper mascot. Most nights she stayed with the other three dogs at the Craig house, with a rumor that she slept on the bed. I was sure she was the most spoiled dog in history.

"It's time for Holly to go outside." I attached her red leash, a gift from Mayor Eva.

"Watch out for the paparazzi," Katy said, and Tammy held up her camera and shot a quick series of me on my way out the door.

While their teasing regularly got old, they were right. I enjoyed the media attention. Since moving to Green, I felt like I had to prove something professionally, and the tornado had allowed me to do that.

Before I got out of the lobby, Linda called me back.

"Phone's for you. Sounds important."

187

I picked Holly up and walked into my office. The caller identified himself as the head of a small chain of regional newspapers, competitors to the newspaper group I had worked for in Ohio.

"We're impressed with your work and would like you to come for a visit."

"That's very gracious of you," I said, "but I don't plan to move away from Green. I not only own the newspaper but I'm married to a local man. This is home for me."

"We'd love to recruit you," the man said with a chuckle, "but I was inviting you to talk about training. Perhaps you've heard about our corporate retreat center."

"The one in Montana?"

"One and the same. How about it? We'd compensate you well for your time."

As he spoke, Holly wandered to the corner and peed. And thus my consulting career was born.

Over supper at the Cotton Boll, I told Chris about the call.

"I committed to make a visit. To Montana."

"Real funny," he said, reaching for the catsup. "You had me going there for a minute."

"I'm serious. They want to wine and dine me at their corporate retreat center in Montana."

"When?"

"Next week."

"How can you possibly do that? You don't have

time to help find us a place to live, much less go to Montana."

"They'll pay me good money, which we sorely need."

"I thought you were settled in Green."

"This is a short business trip, not a job interview."

"But won't it lead to more travel?" he asked. "It sounds to me like they're wooing you for a long-term project."

"They're flexible. They said they'd work around my schedule."

"What about my schedule?"

"That's not fair," I said. "You have summer school and sports, or you could go with me."

"We've only been married three months. I'm not ready to let you go off to kingdom come."

"It's not kingdom come, wherever that is. It's Montana. Out West. Big Sky. You know the place."

"I do know the place. As I recall, we were going there together on our honeymoon." Chris never used that sarcastic tone, and I was shocked.

"I'm going home," I said, "wherever *that* is." I stalked out of the café, barely nodding at the familiar faces between me and the door.

Back at the paper, I took Holly from her crate and got into my car. I drove out to my old home place, sulking from my first fight with Chris since the wedding. "Can't I make my own decisions without consulting him?" I said to the dog. "Doesn't he know how hard it is to make ends meet at the paper?"

The dog whined as though she knew something was wrong.

On Route Two, I held her close and wandered across the land, pulling a lawn chair to the spot where my favorite chair used to sit. Mosquitoes swarmed in the late evening gloom and wasps flitted in and out of a gourd birdhouse. The little house had stayed attached to an oak even though my house had blown away.

"You have no right to take their home," I said, taking off one of my shoes, swatting at the wasps and then running like a crazy person, Holly barking madly.

A sound behind me caught my attention, and I saw Pastor Jean's car drive off. Molly was walking up the driveway.

"Knock, knock," she said with a slight smile. "Is it all right if I come in?"

"If you don't mind hanging out with a person who's crazier than a loon."

"How crazy is a loon?"

"Pretty crazy, apparently. What are you doing way out here?"

"I need to talk to you in private. I caught a ride with Pastor Jean, who was headed this way."

"How'd you know where I was?"

"Jean saw Chris downtown. He told her you two

had a fight, and you weren't at the motel or the paper, so he figured you'd come out here."

"He was right. Let's sit over here." I motioned to the porch swing that Chris had bought me soon after the storm.

"I can't believe it," Molly said, gesturing toward the house. "Where did it all go?"

"Into thin air. Green dust is floating around the country right now."

"Do you think it'll change the places it touches?"

I thought at first she was joking, but the look on her face was serious, almost questioning.

"That's an interesting concept, but that stuff was only stuff. It doesn't live on. It's people who change us, not things."

"That's easier to believe when you have lots of things," Molly said. "Like saying money won't make you happy. Most of the people who say that have money."

I laughed. "That may be true to an extent, but most happiness comes from the heart. People with kind hearts like you are happy. People with money, like Chuck McCuller or Major Wilson, are often miserable, one way or the other."

"You think I have a kind heart?"

"I know you do. You're great with children and animals." I nodded at Holly Beth, now asleep against Molly's chest. "You're one of the few people Kevin trusts to keep Asa. You helped Katy when she was so sad after Matt died, and you help your mother. We're all going to miss you so much when you leave for Florida."

"I'm staying in Green."

"What?" I opened my mouth so wide a gnat flew into it.

"That's what I need to talk to you about. I'm not leaving."

"Molly, we have it all worked out. Your test scores were through the roof, and the scholarship offers are so good. You're going to love Florida."

"Maybe one day," she said. "But I can't leave now. I don't want to. I'm going to a community college in Alexandria. I'll take classes online and I'll only have to drive down there a couple of days a week."

"Are you certain?"

"I am." She stroked the dog.

"Then I hope you'll keep working at the *Item* as many hours as you can."

"Really? I wasn't sure you'd let me." Molly shifted, and Holly Beth whimpered and settled in.

"I'd be crazier than I already am if I didn't let you. Have you told Katy yet?"

"I'm putting that off as long as possible. She's going to kill me. She'll say I'm squandering my talents, but I won't be. I'll be putting them to use in a different way."

Chris's truck pulled into the driveway behind my car, and Kramer and Markey jumped out of the bed in a flash, Mannix coming out a little slower. Holly Beth yelped and ran to greet them, almost dancing in her excitement.

"I'll be right back," I said to Molly and walked quickly to greet my husband with a hug. "I'm so sorry. I won't go if you don't want me to. Green's where I need to be."

"I'm sorry, too. Go and see how this pans out. I never should have gotten angry about it."

"We've got to find a place to live," I said.

"We'll do it when you get back."

"We've only been married three months."

"We've got a lifetime."

The trip to Montana was like a dream.

My cabin had a big screened porch that overlooked a flowing stream. Every piece of furniture had been chosen with the rustic theme in mind, but it was all new and clean.

Corporate employees asked me dozens of questions about motivating a staff and covering a big story with small resources. A high-end cappuccino machine sat on a twig counter near the plank conference table, and we had fresh salads with cranberries and walnuts for lunch.

"What's your management style?" asked a woman whose business-casual outfit looked like what I wore to work on a dressy day.

"It used to be cranky," I said, "but now I'd call it friendly."

"By *friendly,* do you mean *collaborative?*" she asked.

"No, I'm friends with my staff. I do everything the personnel guides say not to do."

"How do you plan big projects, such as the investigative piece you did on political corruption?"

"I ask the staff to handle those. A young reporter named Alex did that project. It resulted in a statewide award for him and jail time for a county official."

"How did you rally your staff for the extra editions you put out after the tornado?" an executive with a beard and glasses asked.

"They rallied me. All of them gathered around me at my wedding reception and got us going. I was stunned by the tornado, but they shook me out of it."

The group seemed to fidget the longer I spoke.

"What advice would you give the leader of a newspaper in a small town?" the first woman asked, and I could see she was doodling squares and circles on a notepad with the company name on it in a typeface that looked like logs.

"Give your heart to the stories, the staff, and the town."

The check for the visit arrived within a week, enough money to pay my monthly note on the *Item*. A typed memo from the president said they enjoyed my "unconventional ideas" but were concerned the strategies would be too difficult to implement on a companywide basis.

"We've decided that hiring you for regular staff development would not work at this time. We wish you all the best."

They called Alex the next week to inquire about his interest in a reporting job.

14

Residents of the Marion community are upset with the placement of a new business that is part gas station, part Mexican restaurant. One of my neighbors said, "Their motto should be, 'Eat here; get gas.'" Their chicken enchiladas are quite tasty, although their gasoline prices are higher than those in town.
—The Green News-Item

When outsiders spoke of Green's fighting spirit, little did they know.

With the raw grief scabbed over, people began to fight about the future.

They argued over zoning, roofers, the lack of treated lumber, and how green Green should be. Constant calls of frustration came from citizens and bureaucrats, and every community correspondent had an idea on the best way for the town to move forward.

"We have always done repairs without permits," said a woman from the garden club. "If I can't get my gazebo rebuilt, I won't be able to host the fall tea."

"Who does that mayor think she is?" another caller demanded. "I need a roof now, not a year from now."

My favorite call came from a woman up in arms over an ice vendor who had opened a small trailer on the edge of town. He supplied contractors, the handful of people still without power, and sportsmen who had given up thinking about the storm and gone fishing.

"I want to file a formal grievance against that ice man," the woman said when I picked up my phone.

"And your reason would be—?" My voice drifted off as I considered how to avoid taking calls in the future. Maybe I'd make Tammy answer my line or let everything roll to voice mail.

"I'm allergic to ice, and I don't appreciate my health being put in jeopardy." I was relieved when she slammed down the phone.

"Lois, someone here to see you," Tammy said, standing with a smirk at my office door the next afternoon. She had resumed her duties at the front counter, and took photographs when another employee was around to handle weddings, obituaries, and the phone. I was ignoring her wedding notices and impending move, now only two months away.

"Send them in."

"He wants you to come outside."

"Major Wilson's not out of jail, is he? Lee Roy Hicks?" Both men had stolen from the paper and done a list of things so wrong I hoped never to see them again. "Chuck McCuller, back from the dead?"

Tammy twirled the end of her hair, which was growing out for her upcoming marriage. "Don't know this dude, but I doubt he's a member of the Country Club set."

When I stepped out, a wiry older man sat at the bottom of the steps on a riding lawn mower, a beer in one hand and a copy of the newspaper in the other, gripped with a bandaged thumb. He had built two small wooden holders on the side of the mower, one for a drink can and the other holding a hammer.

"Is this true?" he asked, holding up the paper.

That afternoon's edition waved in the air, with a main story about an environmental group that wanted to help Green rebuild.

"Yes, sir, it is. The Green Forward group will meet tomorrow with the Police Jury and mayor to discuss what we should do."

"I can tell you what we should do next." His voice was gravelly and weak. "We tell those tree huggers to mind their own business and let us do what we need to do when we need to do it."

The man threw the paper on the ground and took

a sip of beer. "I've never seen such a mess in my life." He ground the mower into gear and pushed the accelerator with a booted foot, picking up surprising speed. Cutting the corner too sharply, he rammed into the recently replaced newspaper rack in the parking lot, leaving it at a haphazard angle. He drove off down Main Street, holding his hand up in an obscene gesture as he went.

"Did he just do what I think he did?" Tammy asked.

"I believe he did," I said. "Stan is going to be so mad about that rack. I'm glad I have you as a witness that I didn't do it."

"Does that count as tornado damage on our insurance claim?" Linda asked, watching the brouhaha from the lobby.

"Everything counts as tornado damage. I think my brain has tornado damage."

Thirty minutes later we got the police call that "some fellow on a riding lawn mower was nailing the doors of City Hall shut." The story made the rounds in record time.

"He told the police he was going to make sure them politicians couldn't get out and ruin people's lives," Linda said. "The chief said he seemed harmless enough, but citizens can't threaten people with hammers. Doug's pretty patient when it comes to the stupids."

"I'm going to see how patient Eva is feeling," I said. "Is she at the courthouse or the store?"

"She was leaving the command center when I went over there this morning," Tammy said. "They're cutting the hours back to half days, three times a week."

The mayor was on the phone in her office at her small department store down the street from the paper, where she had spent most of her time before the storm. Her bob hairdo, a replacement for her helmet of hair from years past, was pushed back with a jeweled clip.

"We need funding and we need it now," she said. "I don't care what fiscal year we're in." She slammed the phone down as I walked in.

"That answers that," I said, slipping into a chair in front of her Oriental desk. "I won the bet on your patience level."

"You don't have a hammer, do you?"

"Do you want to use it on anyone in particular?"

"I'm about ready to use it on every knucklehead who wants to rebuild Green into a jumbled mess and every state official who thinks our tax money belongs to another town."

"So the guy on the tractor had the right idea?"

"I only wish I had thought of it first," she said.

"What do you suggest?"

"We meet as planned tomorrow. We can take an organized, planned strategy and have a great little town, even better than before, or we can throw up our hands and have an unmitigated disaster. The future of Green depends on what we do now."

"Have any idea which way it'll turn out?"

"I'm afraid to think about it. With the highway going full steam, Green may get cut off if we don't get this right."

"I heard the Country Club has reopened for lunch," I said. "How about a little renovation research? I'll put it on my tab."

The next evening, the meeting, held in the high school auditorium, opened politely enough. The Baptist preacher said a prayer and Bud led the Pledge of Allegiance, yet again wearing his volunteer patrol uniform. Eva gave a brief update on the state of Green, followed with a fire department report from Hank and a police report from Doug.

"Our main concern is shoddy construction," Hank said. "If homes aren't wired according to code, we can expect an outbreak of fires. No ifs, ands, or buts." The audience, which included about fifty citizens, several pastors, and every elected official within a fifty-mile radius, mumbled to one another as he spoke.

"The biggest problem in criminal justice," Doug said, "is one we didn't expect. We knew there'd be petty thievery, but there's serious evidence of new meth labs. We're working with the sheriff's department to nip that in the bud."

"Meth labs?" a state legislator said loudly. "What's that all about?"

"We surmise it's because dealers and users think we're too busy to keep an eye on them. I can't elaborate much further. I do want to mention the need for lighting replacement throughout Green. The storm damaged approximately fifty percent of street lights, and that contributes to crime."

By the time Doug had wrapped up his report, it was apparent the air-conditioning was not working. Already mid-July, Green was approaching its hottest days and the air smelled like a school locker room. "You couldn't buy a breeze," Bud had said earlier in the week.

Eva, who I had never seen sweat, returned to the lectern, looking at the back of the room with a smile.

Turning, I saw that Dub had walked in, pushing Joe Sepulvado in a wheelchair. I watched as he maneuvered the chair to the side and slipped into a seat on the back row next to it. This had to top all the things I had experienced since the tornado, even finding Mr. Sepulvado nearly dead. Dub and his brother had let the farmer be unjustly arrested for setting fire to the Dumpster at the newspaper. Now the two looked like old buddies, although Joe was pale and thin.

"We have an ambitious agenda this evening," Eva said, "and I've asked attorney Terrence D'Arbonne from Alexandria to meet with us in case legal issues arise."

The attorney, who had briefly dated Kevin, stood and greeted the crowd, dressed impeccably in a blue blazer and tan slacks, a crisp white shirt, and no tie. "I'm happy to be back in Green. Let me know how I can serve you."

Pastor Jean was next onstage, wiping her brow. "The needs are great. We've seen an outpouring of used clothing and household items, but cash contributions do not nearly cover the requests. While national groups have raised money for victims, overall giving at local churches and nonprofits is down."

"What are you doing about it?" a member of the Bouef Parish Police Jury yelled. "Government can't solve all the problems."

I saw anger wash across Jean's face, but it flashed and disappeared.

"Thank you for the extremely helpful question," she said in what I thought of as her preacher's voice, and the Police Juror fidgeted slightly in his seat.

"Local churches have banded together to track families and collect donations. We're sorting furniture and household goods and finding that God is good at matching gifts with needs."

Pastor Mali, from a downtown church, stood, a big man with a commanding presence and a lyrical accent. He mopped his face with a hand-kerchief, sweat pouring off of him, his dark hair soaking wet.

"Last week a mother with infant twins came to the volunteer center crying. Her children had slept in their car seats since the night of the storm, her trailer was ripped apart. While she was registering, a church member stopped by to say she had two baby beds to donate and did we know of anyone who needed them."

A smattering of applause rippled through the room.

"Praise God," a man said.

"With the leadership of Coach Chris Craig," Jean continued, "we've set up a food distribution program that feeds dozens in rural areas."

"What about food stamps?" a member of the Lakeside Neighborhood Group asked, fanning herself with the agenda. "Aren't they available?"

"We've steered many people to government programs," Pastor Mali said, "but not everyone can produce paperwork to get funds and others are too proud to ask for help. Many elderly people are hurting, because they cannot get to town for help or they do not know how to ask."

"Even though it's been several months, they continue to need food and medicine," Jean said, looking from face to face as though about to give an altar call. "We'll take gently used items, your time, and delivery help . . . and we always appreciate cash."

Laughter followed the last comment, but I felt hollow at the thought of old people alone and I wondered how the children out near where we had found Mr. Sepulvado were doing.

"As these pastors have so eloquently told us, we have many flesh-and-blood needs. We also have been inundated with demands for public projects," Eva said. "We must determine new priorities and decide if we want to pursue additional sources of money."

"Take what we can get," a City Council member shouted out.

"No way, Mayor," Jerry yelled. "We don't want to be obligated to every Tom, Dick, and Harry for how we rebuild our community."

"This is our chance to do it right," someone else said. "It's our only hope of good coming out of this horror."

Eva reached under the lectern and pulled out a hammer. Not a gavel, but a hammer.

"Order," she said, knocking on the wood, garnering laughter from the crowd. "We'll conduct this meeting with dignity, or we will adjourn." She raised the hammer again and everyone laughed more nervously, as though uncertain whether she was serious.

I swiveled in my seat and saw Dub smiling and speaking into Mr. Sepulvado's ear.

Chris had slipped in from summer school wearing Green Rabbits workout clothes. He gave a small wave, and I fanned myself with my hand and mouthed the word, "Help."

He nodded and walked out, back in five minutes with an ice chest of bottled water and a half dozen sweaty football players, who jovially handed water out.

"We will now take questions and civilized comments," Eva said. "Lois Craig will hand the microphone to those with raised hands. Shouting will not be tolerated, and, Lois, I ask you to move on if comments are inappropriate."

This should be fun.

The first question was about the need for a tornado warning system. "Are there legal ramifications for not providing a system?" a City Council member asked.

Terrence stood and took the microphone. "A parish or city is not obligated to provide such a system unless the citizens decide otherwise. I will be back to Green over the next few months holding public hearings on a variety of such issues."

"How about proposed environmental changes?" a representative from the regional economic development association asked.

Several people began to talk at once, and Eva banged the hammer on the lectern so many times that I thought the sturdy wood might fly apart. I was reminded of the first big group meeting I attended in Green, where plans for the new highway were discussed. I could have used a hammer that evening.

"Each individual governmental agency will vote on the 'Make Green Greener' program," Eva said. "I've polled informally and would say it's unlikely the program will be approved."

Some in the audience murmured appreciatively, while others grumbled, but the crowd was quiet within moments. Eva's control was impressive. Terrence took notes on a yellow legal pad.

I passed the mike to the owner of the small feed-and-seed store out toward Route Two. "Will the 'Wide-Awake' rooster be replaced?" he asked, a question that generated more comment than the environmental question. The ten-foot rooster, nicknamed "Doodle," had been blown from a sign welcoming visitors to "Wide-Awake Green."

"We are wide awake," Eva said, "but the fate of Doodle remains to be seen. He was carved by a city employee the year I was born, so he's special to me. You'll have to figure out how old he is." A ripple of laughter went through the hot room.

"I propose we have it recast from fiberglass," the man said. "It's a good promotional tool, and I have it printed on my sacks."

"If you want it so bad, why don't you pay for it?" the snippy Police Juror asked.

"If you'll quit your squawking, I'd be happy to. I'm enlisting with that lady preacher to ask everyone to step up to the plate. What are you going to give?"

The outspoken elected official was suddenly quiet.

"Miss Lois, bring the microphone over here," Bud said and started speaking before I reached him. "I'll order trees to replace the ones we lost. We can have them in time for fall planting season."

"I'll work with Bud on a system for donating trees in memory of people," Anna Grace said. Today she had given up her walker for a cane and she looked cheerful and strong.

"My shop can get flowers for the planters downtown," Becca said.

"I'll water them," Rose, still wearing her sweat-stained mail carrier shirt, said.

Dub raised his hand, and I hesitantly walked to the back of the room. Chris touched his hand to my shoulder and pointed with a grin to Mr. Sepulvado.

I clasped the farmer's hand. "It's wonderful to see you out and about." Once more I wished I knew Spanish.

"*Gracias.*" He returned my smile.

Then I held the microphone for the man I had despised so much.

"I'll make deliveries for those who can't drive," Dub said. "I'll get with the pastors for a list."

"Good man," Mr. Sepulvado said. "Good man."

As the meeting wrapped up, we had resolved a dozen issues, raised a dozen more, and tabled questions that might take years to answer.

The close of the meeting was a surprise to nearly everyone, including me—a video tribute to Green put together and narrated by Katy, using Tammy's photographs.

"In memory of our friend Tom and all those who lost their lives in the tornado," the ending credits said.

Wiping tears from my eyes and considering what Katy's future would look like in broadcasting, I returned the microphone to the stage.

"Good to hear you'll be in Green regularly," I said to Terrence, who stood near the front shaking hands. "Maybe you can go to dinner with me, Chris, and Kevin one evening."

"Since Kevin won't answer my calls, I'd say it's unlikely, but thanks for the thought." He headed across the auditorium, wearing his sport coat even though it was sweltering in the room.

"Excellent work, Mayor," I said, as Eva put her notes in a leather portfolio.

"Overall, this went better than I had hoped," she said.

I did a double take. "Are you sweating?"

15

The Books & Biscuits Club will meet
and eat Thursday evening and discuss
novels that make readers laugh.
The group will also celebrate Trisha Wooley's
birthday, with chocolate cake and a supper
that includes two chicken leg quarters,
baked beans, potato salad, and Texas toast.
"No one will go away hungry, and no one
will go away sad," Virginia Mills promises.
The book club is seeking suggestions for the
next book for the group to read.
—The Green News-Item

Three poster board signs on little sticks lined the driveway to the motel. They looked like those you see in a subdivision for a fortieth birthday, but I couldn't read them until I got much closer.

"Chris & Lois." "Need." "A House."

The words were written in large bubble letters, the handwriting teen girls put on the covers of spiral notebooks. Definitely not designed by Chris.

Cute, real cute was my first thought, followed by a flash of anger at my husband for pulling Katy or Molly into our discussions about where we should live. I stopped so abruptly in front of Unit

Eight that I skidded slightly on the rock parking area.

Our room's door opened, and Chris stood there with a smile, fresh out of the shower, wearing cargo shorts and no shirt. His hair was still wet, and he looked as good as I'd ever seen him look. For a second, I forgot to be aggravated.

"I have a surprise for you," he said, turning around and producing Holly Beth, who had spent the past few days at my in-laws' house. With both of us away for at least twelve hours a day, we juggled Holly from place to place, and I hated it.

I laughed and cuddled the dog. "I've missed the little toot, as your brother calls her."

"She said she's bored out in the country and wants to spend the night in the big city."

"Can she really spend the night?" I sounded like a sixth-grader who desperately wanted a friend to stay over.

"I've got her crate and her toys. We're all set."

He pulled on his shirt and we sat down in the plastic chairs outside the room. I noticed the posters again. "So, what's with the signs? Tell me you haven't stooped that low."

"If you think that's low, why do you think I got Holly? It's July, Lois. We've lived here four months. We have permanently moved into temporary housing."

"But signs in a public place?"

"It's not like the whole town doesn't know that we've homesteaded at the Lakeside." He shrugged. "Katy asked at church where we're going to live. I told her I didn't have a clue. Next thing I know, I pull up and see the signs. You know how she and Molly are."

"They have too much restless energy. They're nervous about college and looking for things to do. Tammy probably had a hand in this too."

"How about we ask them to find us a real place to live? Maybe a home with a yard for the dogs and those modern appliances people cook food on. We need a house."

I put Holly down and watched her chase her tail until she got dizzy and dropped to the grass, ready for a nap.

"I feel like that." I nodded at the dog. "I chase my tail all day and by the time I get here, I want to visit for a while and fall asleep. With the paper and getting ready for football practice and other school details and your food program at church, there's never a spare minute. I haven't been to the antique mall for weeks and I rarely have a real visit with your parents."

"You're rushing too much, Lois."

I reached over and took his hand. "I feel out of control, like the moment the tornado hit. It's as though I'm flying around in the air and everything's whizzing by me."

"A house will help," Chris said. "We'll settle down."

"I miss Route Two and the way things were, your trailer when I turned the corner, the dogs out in the yard, so happy to see me."

"Come here, sweetheart." He stood to hug me.

The crunch of Kevin's tires on the driveway interrupted us, and she let her right window down. "Hey, lovebirds, interesting approach to house hunting," she yelled. "Have you tried looking at For Sale signs in yards? Most people find that helpful."

Chris groaned, and I grinned. She waved and drove on to her parents' apartment behind the office to get Asa.

"That's what I like about staying here," I said, my arm around Chris's waist. "I like to sit at the end of a hard day, not thinking about everything that needs doing."

"But Kevin moved home weeks ago, and Iris has been at Stan's for months. The Taylor house repairs are nearly complete. Most of the other tenants have cleared out, except out-of-town workmen. We're the only ones setting up camp here."

The evening ritual with Pearl, Marcus, and occasionally Kevin had replaced the walks with Chris from the past two years, the late afternoon visits in the newsroom, even the peaceful feeling I used to get when I walked into Grace Chapel with the light streaming through the stained glass windows.

These get-togethers had become a touchstone for me, and I didn't want them to end. I couldn't quite imagine married life any other way.

"School starts in three weeks," Chris said. "I don't see your schedule letting up for months, with the rebuilding coverage and your leadership role on Green Forward. We need a plan."

"Why? So we can watch it get blown to smithereens?"

Lately, I was never quite sure where to find Pastor Jean. Before the storm, I would often find her in her tiny study at the church, preparing a sermon or folding bulletins, or at the parsonage, having a cup of coffee.

When I needed her, she was there.

These days she was a one-woman mission machine, calling on businesses for donations, boxing up necessities for victims, visiting at the hospital and homes, and making sure the school auditorium was ready for our displaced church services each week, complete with an altar. Cell service, erratic before in Green, was now excruciating, so even a chat was tough to arrange. At the makeshift services, she was surrounded by members with needs a mile long. My urge to visit was minor compared to requests for food, a nursing home call, a question about the future of the church.

Her husband, Don, who worked in Baton

Rouge, had stayed for two weeks after the tornado and visited more frequently, moving items from the ruined church into storage. Occasionally I'd see the couple downtown, usually going and coming from one of the bigger churches, where volunteers congregated.

Their marriage seemed to be healing from the tension of her pastoral move to Green, an unforeseen tornado benefit. But I missed Pastor Jean. I missed my personal sermons from her and Kids' Club on Wednesday nights and the shoving at the buffet line and the way the little church looked, sitting there on the corner near my house, a classic white frame building with a steeple and a bell that my father-in-law had rung for sixty years.

Now we met in the school auditorium. I knew where I worshiped shouldn't matter, but it did. Not only were the seats uncomfortable, I couldn't turn my brain off and focus on the message, worrying instead about what needed to be done.

It was time to track Jean down and cry on her shoulder; the Tuesday afternoon paper was on its way to homes, delivery almost back on schedule.

"Do you ever sleep?" I asked when I found her putting boxes together alone in a storeroom at the Methodist church near the paper. She had on jeans, a little too big for her, and a youth camp T-shirt with a hole in it. Her eyes had circles under them.

"Sleep? What's that?" She kept trying to fit the pieces of the box together, unable to get the sides to meet, her hands shaking. "These darned things are not user-friendly."

"Let me help you."

And she burst into tears.

Jean had shed a tear or two in front of me over the past two and a half years, but this was crying like I'd seldom seen. My eyes widened, and I tried to take the box from her hands, but she wouldn't let go.

"I've got to finish these boxes before three," she said, "when the volunteers come get them. I should already have them done, but I can't get them to work right." She held the box, no longer trying to put it together but not laying it down.

"Jean, you're worn out. Get someone else to do this, and I'll take you home for a nap."

"There isn't anyone else. Everyone has more to do than they can handle."

"At least take a break. I'll get you a cup of that strong coffee you love so much, and you can rest for a little while."

Still she clung to the box.

"I'll be right back." I wandered down the halls of the pretty, old church, knowing someone somewhere would have coffee. The scorched smell of a nearly empty pot led me to a small kitchen, and I rummaged around until I found two Styrofoam cups, lumpy creamer, and a box of sugar cubes. I tucked the entire box under my arm, knowing Jean liked lots of sugar in her coffee.

"Find everything you need?" a voice asked

behind me, and I jumped, dropping the sugar cubes, which spilled out on the vinyl floor.

"Pastor Mali!" I exclaimed, sounding slightly wild to my own ears. "You caught me! I'm stealing from the Methodists."

"What's ours is yours. Are you OK, Miss Lois?" A look of pure concern appeared on his face. He had bags under his eyes, too, and a look of strain around his mouth, similar to what I had seen on Jean's face.

"I'm visiting Pastor Jean." I held up the coffee. "She needs caffeine and lots of it."

"Most of all she needs a friend," he said, helping me pick up the sugar cubes.

When I opened the door to the storeroom, Jean was back at work putting boxes together and had made considerable progress in the few minutes I'd been gone. We sat on cartons of canned goods and drank the coffee in silence for a few moments.

"The state is pushing harder to buy the church land for the highway," Jean said finally. "All of it, not only the parsonage plot but the church, too. They also want Maria's place."

I gulped, the horrible weak coffee scalding my throat.

"Did you tell them it wasn't for sale?"

"I told them I would pray about it. And talk to the congregation."

"Grace Community has been on that corner for decades. It's a landmark," I said.

"You know we were worried about how close the highway was coming. We were going to have to make a decision."

"But move the church? That was never mentioned."

"We didn't face a massive renovation challenge when we first spoke of it. The insurance company says it'd be cheaper to tear the old building down and build a new one. Hank says it'd be much easier for a new building to meet safety and accessibility codes."

"What about the cemetery, where Chris's first wife and Iris's son are buried?"

"The state would fence it, make it accessible from the other side."

"Can we wait a few months to decide?" I asked. "Things are so up in the air."

"The Department of Transportation wants an answer in twenty-one days, and us out of the parsonage within two months. They've pushed me since the storm, but I've been too busy to think about it. The church trustees are not going to be happy when they find out I didn't tell them sooner."

"You've been helping people. That's the kind of pastor you are, Jean. You care more about hearts than bricks."

"Oh, Lois," Jean said, "I'm tired, and there's so much to do."

"You've got to take care of yourself or you won't be able to help anyone."

"So many people need help. I feel guilty whining to you. I thought things were bad before the storm, but we're working from scratch here."

"Hmmm." I put my head in my hands.

"What are you doing?" she asked with a shaky laugh.

"I'm trying to think what my pastor would tell me."

"She would probably—"

"Shhh. Breathe for a minute."

We sat in the dim room, surrounded by unopened boxes of pinto beans and rice and canned corn, stacks of cardboard waiting to become boxes, and the dozen containers Jean had put together earlier. Outside I could hear the sound of a chain saw and distant hammering.

I reached for Jean's hand, thinking of the many times she had encouraged me, the way she had steadied me when my faith was weak.

"Even Jesus took time off," I said. "He had people to heal and sermons to preach and all those sheep you're always telling me about. He went away to pray and catch his breath."

"Catch his breath," she said. "That must be the gospel according to Lois. If you're still offering, I think I'll take you up on that ride home."

After settling Jean in what she called her prayer chair in the living room, I took a casserole, a loaf of bread, and a cobbler out of her freezer on the carport and put them in her oven. One thing Jean never lacked was homemade meals, ready to heat and eat, gifts from the people of Grace. They had quickly replaced her supplies when the power came back.

She was asleep by the time I looked in on her.

Setting the timer on the forty-year-old white stove, one of several things that needed updating in the parsonage, I stepped outside and surveyed the broken-down church. The roof sagged more, and the steeple lay perilously close to Jean's front wall. I walked across the driveway and opened the front door, swollen and requiring a hard tug. The smell of mold hit my nose, and a field mouse skittered into the choir loft.

Two of the beautiful stained glass windows were cracked near the ceiling, but the others were unharmed. The glass vases of tulips from our wedding remained on each ledge, the flowers withered and the water dried up.

I knew at that moment we would never worship here again.

Maria and her sons were in the yard when I came out of the church, my eyes wet with tears.

"*Hola*, Miss Lois," she called, and the boys waved shyly, wearing swimsuits and playing in the sprinkler. I walked across the gravel road, trying to pull myself together, the boys going back to a game of chase, timing their moves to coincide with the arc of the water.

"You have heard the news?" Maria asked hesitantly.

"News?" I was shifting from my good-bye to the old church to the exuberance of the kids, thrilled to see them with a yard to play in.

"About the government. A man came by and said we must find a new place to live. They are taking our home."

"Maria, this is the United States. They can't kick you out of your house."

"One moment. I have an official letter for Mr. Chris. It arrived yesterday."

I sat on the front steps and opened the fat white envelope, finding a complicated three-page letter and a thick contract. "In light of changes rendered by the tornado of twenty-six March, revisions are hereby made to proposed highway project number 691980, affording the opportunity for the sale of your land at appraised market value within sixty days."

Who got paid to write these things?

The state must think Chris still owned the property and want him to sell out. The words had a slightly ominous tone to them.

"My boys love this home so much. I told them we would not have to move again for a long time. Where will we go?" Maria asked.

"We can fight this."

"But the church must move too. The road will be there." She pointed to the corner.

She was right. A fight would be a waste of energy that none of us had. The church would find a new site and rebuild. Maria and the boys didn't need to be in the shadow of a four-lane road.

"We'll look for new land and move this for you," I said, not having a clue where we might put the trailer. "They don't call them mobile homes for nothing."

She looked at me quizzically, clearly not understanding a word I said.

"We'll find a better place." I worked up my most enthusiastic voice. "It'll be another adventure. Don't worry about anything. Everything is going to be all right."

Easing back into Jean's house, I peeked into the living room where she was sound asleep, a hint of a snore coming from her mouth.

Breathing in the hominess of her kitchen, I took the food from the oven, dished a serving of the casserole onto a bright yellow Fiestaware plate and put the cobbler in a red bowl. I made a small salad with a wilted head of lettuce, figuring Jean needed a vegetable, quietly poured a glass of tea, and broke a piece of bread.

A sudden image of Jean serving the Lord's Supper flashed into my mind.

"Do not let your hearts be troubled," I heard her saying, the lovely Grace Chapel glowing with morning light.

16

*Cody Rigdon is recovering at home
after falling out of the back of his friend
Brandon's new Chevy pickup. "A handful
of boys were horsing around out in the
country. Cody decided to stand up in the bed
of the truck at the same time Brandon
swerved to avoid a skunk," Cody's dad said.
"We've warned him about that before,
but I think he learned his lesson this time.
He'll be working the next four summers to
pay off that emergency room bill."*
—The Green News-Item

On the first Sunday in August, we ate lunch as usual with Estelle and Hugh, and Chris settled down to watch football videos, a task he seemed never to tire of.

I sat in his lap and kissed his neck.

"I have a surprise for you," I said.

"Here?" He actually blushed and glanced around. "Where are Mama and Daddy?"

"Not that kind of surprise. I have a list of houses for us to look at. I've stalled long enough."

"That's great news." He reached for my notebook. "Let's see what you've found."

I held the list out of reach, swinging it by the metal coil at the top. "No, no, no. I've got our itinerary all mapped out. Let's go for a Sunday drive."

Chris's truck seat was cluttered with a case of water, a map of the parish, country roads highlighted with a marker, and a list of people who needed food, so we climbed into my small car, me in the driver's seat, Chris complaining about how low to the ground it sat.

"We could take your truck if it hadn't become a mobile food bank," I said.

"I don't think I'll ever get caught up. This food business was supposed to have eased up by now, but the more people hear about it, the more requests we receive."

"Give yourself the afternoon off." I was astonished to find myself energized at the prospect of locating a home. "Even though Green doesn't have a lot of neighborhoods to choose from, I ruled out the area around the Country Club. Those houses are dated, and I don't like the thought of living there. The houses in the new development by the school are jammed together, so I put that area on the long list."

"You're telling me we have to live at the Lakeside for the rest of our marriage, aren't you?"

"I have three excellent ideas, so prepare to be wowed."

The first house was a small white frame cottage in Kevin's neighborhood with a patched roof and a cute picket fence. "The neighborhood's a little uneven, but we could put our money where our mouth is and support this area," Chris said.

We got out of the car and walked around the yard.

"It's vacant, but it's been partially restored," I said.

He pointed to boards pulling away from the front windows and the tilt of the tiny cement porch, a wrought iron post pulled out at the bottom.

"Apparently my idea of partially restored and theirs are two different things," I said.

"Good idea to consider this neighborhood," Chris said, "but wrong house."

I made an elaborate show of crossing the address off my list, and Chris tried to read over my shoulder.

"No peeking. This is the Lois Craig real estate tour."

He crawled into my car, his long legs crowded in the tight space. "Next?"

"Iris and Stan are talking about building, but there's another option." I drove to the south side of town. "What if we moved one of these houses onto Aunt Helen's lot?"

We pulled into a dealer who sold houses that were a combination of prefabricated and custom-built, a variety of architectural styles. "What do you think?"

"Interesting idea," he said. "I stopped by here a

couple of weeks ago. They have several good-looking model homes."

"They're cute, too," I said.

"I'm not sure I want to live in a cute house."

"Charming, then. I wouldn't have considered this a year or two ago, but now it seems like one of our easier options. Let's look around."

The sales manager made a beeline for us as soon as we stepped from the car.

"Good to see you, Coach, Miss Lois," he said. "I hoped you'd be back together."

I glanced at Chris, sheepish. "I came over here last week too."

As we explored the model homes, we discussed the pros and cons of a new house at the old home place.

"Would it look out of place?" I asked.

"Depends on the style," Chris said.

"Would we be too close to the highway?"

"Not from the revised plans that your newspaper posted online. There's a big slice of land behind the parsonage and then all those trees on your land. That's probably ten acres or more."

"What about construction and traffic noise? Iris is concerned about that."

"I don't think they'll be able to see the interchange from her house, and I know we wouldn't on your land."

"Our land," I said.

"Our land," he repeated.

"It'll be different without the church and your old trailer there. It won't feel like as much of a community, but I guess I have to get used to that idea."

"It'll be a new community," Chris said. "Our lot is not too far from the spot Pastor Jean has picked out for the new church. She hopes we can move Maria and the boys to a spot down that way too. She's found an acre of land near the little store there at the crossroads. Now she has to decide about a parsonage."

We strolled through three model homes, pushing the salesman off on a family who pulled in behind us. "We're having a look," Chris said. "We'll give you a shout if we have any questions."

The floor plans were much more efficient than in the old house where I had lived, complete with laundry rooms, electric fireplaces, and garden tubs in the master bathrooms. The windows were insulated and opened easily, and the doors shut snugly.

I thought of the front screened porch at Aunt Helen's, the pitch of the roof with intricate woodwork, the tall brick chimney, glass doorknobs, and claw-foot bathtub. "They don't have as much personality as an old house, but we could probably replace the deck with a porch."

"There'd be a lot less maintenance," Chris said.

"We could choose interesting colors and decorate them in our style."

"Thank goodness I put most of my catfish collection in Mama's attic," Chris said.

"Please tell me that while half of Bouef Parish blew away, the catfish collection doesn't live on."

"It's available if needed, Mrs. Craig. We can make it the cornerstone of the décor."

"You're keeping secrets. I thought you gave all that to the shelter."

He grinned, his cute Chris grin. "I didn't figure they'd want that stuff."

"At least we have the piece of green pottery you recovered. That's a start. Rose can help us find antiques, too. Linda's been too busy to do much with the shop, but Rose is back to regular hours at the Holey Moley."

"This is a good floor plan," Chris said. "We could have our room here, and the children over here."

My eyebrows shot up. Before we got married, we had discussed possibly having a child one day, but the topic had not been raised since.

"Are we house shopping or family planning?" I asked.

"Just in case. This could be the children's room, just in case. These models would be ideal in a lot of ways, but they're not quite what I had in mind."

"Me either." I was relieved at his opinion and the change of subject.

"We could build a brand-new house," he said. "That's a lot of work, but it could be fun. Maybe more expensive than we planned."

"Before we discuss building, I have one more for us to look at today. It's a little extreme, but promise you'll give it a chance."

"If you like it, I'll give it a chance, whatever it is, wherever it is."

"It's on the lake, in the older part of Major Wilson's development. I vowed I'd never buy over there, but the listing sounds perfect, and the pictures look like it's ready to move right in. It has the master suite on one side and guestrooms—or a nursery—on the other."

A strange look passed across Chris's face.

"What's wrong? I thought you might like living on the lake. The lots are big, and we could even get a boat. They're having an open house today, so we can look around without an appointment."

"Let's take a look," he said. "It can't hurt."

"I'm so relieved that I'm finally excited about looking at a house."

The drive through the brick gates was a transition into another world from Route Two. Most homes had a view of the water, many had piers and boathouses. A row of smaller patio homes sat to the left of the entrance, expensive replicas of Creole cottages with cypress beams and antique brick walkways.

We wound to the back. "Here's the turn," I said. "Even the street has a cute name. How could you not be happy in a house on Bluebird Lane?"

I glanced at my notes and back at the brass numbers on the door. "This is it. It looks better in person. Isn't it darling?"

I was almost to the front door before I noticed Chris wasn't moving. His car door was open, and he had both feet on the ground but he didn't seem to have any momentum.

"Come on, slowpoke," I yelled. "They're going to close at four."

He stepped out of the car and leaned against the front fender, his hand on the hood as though to hold himself up.

"Lois." His quiet voice seemed to reverberate across the yard. "I know what it looks like. This was my and Fran's house."

I took a step toward Chris and then turned back to the house, looking at it as though I'd never seen a house before. A young woman with a real estate nametag came to the door and invited me in. "It's stunning," she said. "The original owners were quite creative with the design."

"I'm stunned all right," I mumbled, feeling as though I might throw up. "Excuse me."

Chris and I got in the car and made the short drive back to the motel in silence, except for an occasional sniffle from me and one heavy sigh from Chris.

When I pulled into the parking spot, I didn't know what to do. Part of me wanted to push Chris out of the car and run away. Another wanted him to explain why he had never mentioned a house on the lake.

He spoke first. "I'm so sorry. I never meant to mislead you."

"That's obvious," I said in my most sarcastic tone, a good dose of hurt mixed in. "You made me think you and Fran lived in the trailer on Route Two. Not one time has a house on the lake been mentioned, not one time."

"Can we go inside to talk about this? My legs are cramping."

"You go. I've got work to do at the paper." I put the car in reverse, but he didn't move.

"I'm not getting out of the car without you," he said in a subdued voice.

I started driving. "Well, I guess you can go to the *Item* with me."

"Can we at least talk about this rationally?"

Hearing my husband of four months imply I was irrational added fury to my emotions. I drove too fast down Main Street, largely empty on a Sunday afternoon, and whipped into the *News-Item* parking lot, swinging wide, and flattening the newspaper box.

I had never heard Chris utter a curse word, not even in the middle of the tornado, but I think he came close at that moment.

230

I put my head on the steering wheel, hiding my face.

"Let me try to explain," he said.

"I thought I knew you."

"I thought I knew you, too. I had no idea you had delusions of being a NASCAR driver."

"This isn't a joking matter."

"I suspect Stan will agree with you on that. How many times have you flattened that rack?"

"I'm going inside. You can do whatever you want to do."

"Could you take me to get my truck?" he asked. "We left it at my parents' house."

For a moment I considered telling him to walk. "I guess so."

"May I drive?" he asked.

I didn't answer but walked around the car, my knees trembling.

We met at the trunk, and he reached up and touched my hair, one of his most tender gestures.

"I love you, Lois. You make me happier than I ever expected to be. You make me happy even when a tornado hits." He tried to hug me, but I stood rigid, not nearly ready to yield to his sweetness.

We pulled out. Again the drive was silent, me staring out the window, feeling betrayed.

Before I realized where he was going, we pulled into the driveway where the cottage had stood. The birds seemed to be singing extra loudly. More than anything I wanted to run into the old house and throw myself on my bed, sinking into my beautiful new down comforter and feeling the cool pillow under my head. But all that was wiped out.

We walked over to the swing and sat down. "I don't suppose we can let this go?" Chris asked.

I didn't say anything, wondering what planet he was from.

"Are you going to talk to me?" he asked.

I crossed my arms, ever-so-slightly enjoying watching him squirm.

"Lois, I'm sorry. I don't know what else to say."

"How about telling me what else I don't know about you? How about explaining why no one in town ever mentioned a fancy lake house, Mr. I-love-the-stars-and-open-space?"

"I wasn't trying to hide it from you. At first, it didn't seem relevant. We weren't dating, so I let it slide. Later I knew it bothered you to talk about Fran, so I didn't know how to bring it up."

"It's hard to think about you being married to another woman," I said. "To find out you lived in that beautiful house. . . . It's like learning there's a side to you I never had an inkling of."

"Fran was a wonderful wife—"

"Thanks for reminding me."

"Let me finish. She was a wonderful wife, but she didn't much like the country. That was her dream house, and it meant more to her than it did to me."

"Did you build it yourselves?"

"We did. I said I'd never do that again, but I'd do it in a minute if that's what you want. You're the best thing that ever happened to me. I sort of always knew I'd marry Fran from the time we were in high school, but you, you caught me off guard. You were an unexpected gift."

I looked over at the house site, remembered sitting on the porch, risking my heart to a man who had loved deeply before, remembered Chris's willingness to risk his heart again.

"I should have known Fran never lived in that mobile home," I said.

He was ill at ease, and the out-of-left-field comment threw him. "I'm not following you."

"She would never have put up with that catfish skull in the bathroom."

"That was all me." Chris offered a half smile.

"I'm not sure if that makes me feel better or not. But I'm not throwing you back."

"Are we OK then?" He put his arm across the back of the swing, the way we had sat so many times while getting acquainted.

"I suppose so, but we still don't have a place to live . . . and no more secrets."

"Let me show you one more house possibility," he said. "It's a long shot, but it's been on my mind."

Chris drove, taking a left out of the driveway, away from Grace Chapel and town, and headed west past the monument to the boll weevil, a reminder of Green's unending economic challenges, making another turn about ten miles later onto a small paved road.

"I've never been way out here," I said.

"I hope this go-cart of yours can make it." Chris swerved to miss a pothole. "This is my parents' land." He made another turn, down a grown-up, rutted drive.

A weather-beaten Louisiana-style house, similar to Helen's, sat covered in vines, trees up to the porch.

"This was my grandmother's house."

A snake slithered into the tall grass as I got out of the car, and Chris had to pull me up onto the porch, the steps long gone. "Watch your step. Most of this is rotten."

"Great." I gingerly stepped over a cracked board, trying to keep my balance.

He pulled a skeleton key out of his pocket. "Believe it or not, the front door stays locked."

"From the looks of things, vandals have found other ways in." I stayed close to Chris.

"There used to be a screened door here, but someone stole it a few years ago. Daddy always thought it was funny that they took the screened door and not the antique wooden one."

"It's a work of art. I've never seen such a beautiful door in my life." It had four different colored stained glass panes, in rich colors you

234

seldom saw in modern glass. The bottom had a four-panel design with dogwood blooms carved on every panel.

Chris gave the door a shove to unwedge it. "The house has settled," he said. "It'd have to be leveled, among other things."

We stepped into a wide hall that went straight to the back of the house.

"It started off as a dogtrot," he said. "All the rooms open off this hall, and the kitchen and the side porch were added through the years."

Peeling pink and gray floral wallpaper was torn back, revealing a fabric that resembled cheesecloth over wide boards. The ceiling was made from beaded board, and the windows were largely intact, huge old glass that showed bubbles in the afternoon sun.

The entire time I oohed and aahed over its details, I fluctuated between thinking how pale the prefab houses looked compared to this and wondering how you breathed new life into a long abandoned house.

"This was grandma and grandpa's bedroom, and here is the living room." Chris walked to the other side of the hall. An old wood-burning stove sat in the corner, a pipe running out the window.

"Here's Grandma's sewing room, and the dining area and kitchen. The kids always had to eat out there." He pointed to the little porch, lined with windows.

"Look at this piece of furniture." I touched a screened door on the front of a cupboard. I heard a creature scurry inside it, and I stepped back so quickly I bumped into Chris.

"That was Grandma Craig's pie safe. I forgot it was out here. Now that I look around, it's probably the only thing salvageable about the whole thing, that and the front door."

He steered me back toward the front. "It would cost a fortune to remodel this place, even if we did the work ourselves, which we don't have time to do. We could build a brand-new place for what we could fix this one up."

"It is awfully far out here. But it sure has a lot of character."

17

Candy and Cookie Sheridan's vegetarian cooking class has been postponed until after Christmas, due to insufficient registration. "We look forward to explaining the myths surrounding protein in main dishes," Cookie said. However, county agent Toby Howell says he has added an additional session to his upcoming free Wild Game Preparation and Cooking seminar. He requests students bring their own game.
—The Green News-Item

Alex gave his notice on the Monday after the house-hunting trip, the week before Katy and Molly headed to college, and a month before Tammy's wedding.

I could barely listen for scratching the redbug bites accumulated while walking through the grass at Chris's grandmother's house.

They were especially bad behind my knees and where I had worn short socks with tennis shoes. Thank goodness I hadn't been in my sandals, recently bought from Eva's department store as I began to replenish my wardrobe.

"Will two weeks be enough notice?" Alex asked.

I dabbed calamine lotion on my arms where I had gotten a nasty case of poison ivy.

"Two years won't be enough. Plus, it's hard to concentrate on my best reporter leaving when I'm itching to death. I don't want to talk about it."

"Your best reporter? I'm your only real reporter."

"I thought you turned down those job offers."

"I did at first. West News, that chain where you did the consulting, came back with a better offer. I'll be the news service reporter in three states. Apparently they like the things you told them."

"That must be why they never called me back."

"You may have been a little, well, offbeat for them."

"Offbeat? I'm a rule follower. I do things by the book."

"Maybe you used to, but you do things different down here in Green," Alex said. "Plus, you gave the impression you weren't interested. The editor in Boise said you were casual in your presentation and made it clear you had too many commitments in Louisiana to do the kind of travel they wanted."

"I did?" I tried not to claw my armpits in front of him.

"They're super impressed with what the paper's doing. They say our coverage is better than most of the big guys, even though they can't quite figure out how you make it all work."

"Can't you wait till next year?" I felt guilty preying on his conscience, but I didn't know what

I was going to do. I was soon to have a staff of three. If I was lucky, and Molly could work out her schedule, I might have three and a half.

"They've about run out of patience with me. I put them off before, and it's now or never."

"Are you sure you want to live out West?" *And make twice as much money and see the country and go to training sessions at that cool retreat center?*

"I'm young and single, so I figure the timing's right. I could never have gotten this job without you. You taught me way more than I learned in J-school."

For a minute, I forgot the itching.

"You've done a fantastic job, Alex. At my former paper, I'd send my staff off with wishes for a great future. But it's hard to let you go."

"It's hard to go." He wiped at his eyes surreptitiously when he reached the door. "Is poison ivy contagious?"

I heard whooping and hollering from the newsroom, and I hobbled in there, not sure if it was the dried pink lotion, the bites, or Alex's announcement that had paralyzed me.

"Oh, my," Tammy said. "You are eat up with redbugs."

"Is that poison ivy?" Iris Jo asked, backing off. "I'm too close to finishing my chemo to get covered up with that stuff."

"What are we going to do?" Katy moaned.

"It's not leprosy," I said. "I'm sure it'll go away in a few days."

"I mean about Alex," she said.

"*We* aren't going to do anything. If memory serves me correctly, this time next month, you'll be on your way to become a television commentator."

"Reporter," Katy snapped. "I'm not trying to be an anchor. Maybe I shouldn't go. Maybe I should stay here and help out."

A tiny feeling of temptation ran through me, but I knew it wasn't right.

"Under no circumstances are you staying. Maybe we'll let you work here next summer, if a highfalutin television station doesn't grab you."

"First Tom and now Alex," Katy said.

"I'm not dying," Alex said, sitting on the edge of his desk. "I'm moving to Idaho."

"Might as well be dead," the intern said. "We'll never see you again." I used to worry about Alex flirting with Katy. She had turned eighteen two weeks ago, and I thought they might have gone on a date to mark the occasion.

"I'll be back. Or you can visit me."

Molly breezed through the lobby wearing her smock from the convenience store where she worked evenings and most Saturdays. She stopped so suddenly her tennis shoes made a squeaking noise.

"Why does everyone look so serious?" she

asked, stepping into the newsroom, and then looked at me. "Is that poison ivy?"

"It's a designer mixture of redbugs and poison ivy," I said.

"Alex is leaving," Katy said. "He took that job out West." Molly rushed over to Katy to console her and then gave Alex a hug.

"Miss Lois," Molly said, echoing Katy's question, "what are we going to do?"

"We'll figure it out. Don't forget the staff party at the Country Club next week. We've got lots to celebrate—college, a wedding, the end of Iris Jo's chemo, and a bon voyage. Now if you'll excuse me, I think it's time for another lotion application."

When I got into my office, I pulled out Aunt Helen's typewritten history of the newspaper, seeking insight.

Iris slipped in quietly. "This could be an answer to part of our financial problems," she said. "Alex is our highest paid employee, which isn't saying much, but it will help."

"How can we be a newspaper without news?"

"Linda's ready, and you know it," Iris said. "She can step in for Alex in a heartbeat. Molly can do Tom's layout work. I'm stronger now, so I'll take over all the accounting and some of the advertising. You can help with the rest of the advertising."

"I'm not a salesperson."

"You've called on all the big accounts for nearly three years now."

"Have you been taking bossy lessons from me?"

"You know I don't like bossing, but we need to tighten our belts."

"If we tighten them any more, we'll have to close the doors.

"Who's going to write editorials?" I asked.

"You and Linda."

"Who's going to take pictures after Tammy gets married?"

"You and Linda."

"I was afraid you were going to say that."

We kept the celebration dinner small, adding only a handful of correspondents to the staff guest list.

Katy came in holding hands with Alex, although she pulled away the moment they entered the small reserved dining room.

Molly brought a young man who looked vaguely familiar, and I finally placed him as the football player she had talked to the first time I went to a Rabbits game. His clothes were slightly worn but clean, and his shoes looked like they were two sizes too small. He practically limped as Molly led him into the small party room.

"Coach," he said, holding out his hand. "Mrs. Craig. Thank you for having me."

"Thank Molly." I shook his hand. "She's the star."

Molly beamed.

The two walked over to where Alex and Katy stood with Iris and Stan.

"What's his story?" I asked Chris, who had refused to wear a tie to the function but looked cute in a blue shirt and khakis.

"That's Anthony Cox, the kid who lives out where we found Mr. Sepulvado."

"In that house that's falling down, the one with the little sister and the baby?"

"That's him. He's got great potential as a player and he's a solid student. I have high hopes for him. He has another year of high school because he missed a year when he was in grade school. His mother moved and never got him enrolled or something strange like that."

Bud escorted Anna Grace into the room, no cane or walker in sight. She did, however, seem to be leaning heavily on his arm. A widower since January, Bud, at least ten years younger than Anna Grace, had a spring in his step that I had never seen. Tonight he wore slacks and a knit shirt, his volunteer police uniform apparently in storage for the evening.

"I hope you won't think less of us," Anna Grace said, "but Bud and I are dating."

"Now why in the world would I think less of you?"

"His wife only passed away seven months ago, but we're not getting any younger. After my incident at your wedding reception, he finally took notice."

"That's pretty dramatic flirting, Anna Grace. In most cases an ambulance is not required."

"A woman's got to do what a woman's got to do. I even got him to buy a laptop. You should see the e-mails he sends me. They're quite clever."

Last year we had led Bud and others kicking and screaming into the digital age. Now he was courting online?

Before I could get my mind around that concept, in walked Linda with Doug, the police chief. "It's not a date," she said when I dragged her to the side of the room, "but I couldn't bear to come alone. I hope you don't mind that I brought a source."

In my days in Dayton, dating a source would have been cause for a reprimand or a personnel powwow. Tonight it felt as though Linda had made another move forward on her journey. She had been divorced from an abusive husband for years and held back from the group on most occasions.

Tammy whooshed into the room, carrying her camera as always, Walt following in her wake.

"Thank goodness," Linda said, heading back to Doug. "Perfect timing to get your attention off me. The queen bee herself."

I walked over to Chris, leaning against the wall, taking it all in. "It's only a little while till their wedding," I said. "Walt looks dazed."

"I know the feeling," Chris said.

"Not long now," I said to Walt.

"Can't get here soon enough," Walt said, shaking hands with Chris and giving me a peck on the cheek.

"Are you sure we can't twist your arm into coming?" Tammy asked. "We've got a beautiful beach house rented for family and friends."

"You don't want us at your wedding," I said. "Does the word *hurricane* mean anything to you? Besides, if Chris and I don't find a house soon, my husband will be looking for a new wife."

"The only thing that sounds better than a vacation to Florida is a house with more than one room," Chris said. "But Lois sure is going to miss you."

"I'm only going to be on vacation for two weeks," Tammy said. "One week for the wedding and one for the cruise."

"You're coming back?" I suspected my expression was thunderstruck.

"Of course I'm coming back. Were you going to fire me for getting married?"

"We all assumed you wouldn't make the drive from Shreveport. It's been so wild that we haven't—" My voice trailed off.

"I'm learning how to be a photojournalist," Tammy said. "Surely you didn't think I'd become one of those ladies who lunch or play tennis on weekday mornings?"

"That sounds enjoyable. Are you sure?"

"The only people I know in Shreveport are Walt's parents and a few snooty women I met at his country club. It's not nearly as friendly as this one."

"We found a house south of Shreveport," Walt said. "It's a shorter commute for Tammy, and I can work at home if I want to."

"I was going to ask you about a four-day week," Tammy said, fidgeting with the blue glass beads she wore. "I read that it's called flex time."

"That's the most wonderful idea I've heard in months," I said. Stan and Iris walked up to see what I was laughing about. "Did you hear that, Iris? Tammy's not leaving us after all."

"I told you this would work out," Iris said. "You're going to love married life, Tammy. It's the best."

Chris gave me a look that I would walk through fire to see. "It certainly is," he said.

The evening was filled with toasts and roasts and more than a few tears.

"No excessive partying at the University of Georgia," I told Katy, "and remember that people around here root for LSU. No speeding to Alexandria," I said to Molly. "You two girls have reminded me how journalism is supposed to work." I handed them each a framed page of the first tornado extra and a gift card.

I turned to Alex. "Keep making them think we're smart down here. We couldn't have gotten where we are without you." I gave him a leather notebook with his name embossed on the front. "Comfort the afflicted and afflict the comfortable, and never forget that citizens have a right to know."

I saw Katy reach over and squeeze his hand.

"To Tammy and Walt, may your marriage be picture perfect." I handed Tammy a high-end digital camera, bought with bonus points from one of the *Item*'s credit cards. "I can't wait to see how you develop."

The small group laughed.

"To a woman of faith and strength, Iris Jo." My eyes welled up. I pulled out a beautiful pink blown glass vase I'd found at Rose's shop. "To your victory over cancer. And your marriage, which came on the day we needed it most."

I lifted Tom's green eyeshade. "Finally, to the most courageous of all, Tom, who gave his life trying to warn us about the storm. He's the least likely angel I ever met, and yet I feel him looking over my shoulder every single day."

"To Tom!" Katy said. "To Tom!" yelled Alex. "To Tom!" Linda cried. And around the table we went, saluting the curmudgeonly copy editor who had touched each of us.

I could barely stand for the evening to end.

"This will look wonderful in our new home,"

Iris Jo said, walking over to where I stood in a corner, gazing at the staff.

"We're going to tear down the old place," Stan said, "and rebuild a house with all the environmental bells and whistles. We'll show those highway people how it's done."

"We liked the ideas thrown around at the town meeting," Iris said, "and we want to give them a try. Stan's found all sorts of resources on the Internet."

"You're moving back to Route Two?" I asked, my upbeat heart cracking a little.

"We hope to be moved within the year," Iris said. "How about you and Chris?"

"We don't know yet. We may build out there or we may keep looking."

Waiting for Chris to pull his rusty truck around to the front of the club, I saw Mayor Eva, Dub, and Joe Sepulvado all walking out of the dining room, Eva holding on to Dub's arm.

"No more wheelchair," I said to Joe.

"All well," he said.

"As long as he doesn't overdo it," Dub said.

"As though Dub would let that happen," Eva said.

They were an interesting group, that was for sure.

"So they finally let you out of the bunker," I said to Eva.

"And you as well. You're looking perky tonight. Did I see that outfit in my store earlier this week?"

"You did indeed. The honeymoon clothes were getting a little dingy."

"That shade of orange is the perfect color for you," she said. "I hope we gave you the tornado discount."

I smiled and turned back to Mr. Sepulvado. "Chris and I have been meaning to get in touch with you. Have you found a place to live?"

"I'm staying with Mr. McCuller here," the Mexican immigrant said in his heavy Spanish accent. "My bedroom is bigger than our trailer was."

"Why, Dub, what a nice gesture." Astonishment overrode disdain in my voice.

"I have plenty of room," Dub said, "and Joe needed a place. Not a big deal."

"It eases the loneliness," Mr. Sepulvado said. "I miss my wife, and the children can't afford to come to Green. Dr. Kevin says I should not go back to Mexico until I get stronger."

Chris pulled up at the curb, his truck a stark contrast to Eva's new Cadillac, brought around next. He got out and shook hands with the threesome. "Joe, you're looking *bueno*. We hope to get the Spanish service going again within the month. Sure hope to see you then."

"Maybe this fellow will come with me," Mr. Sepulvado said, pointing to Dub. "He's picked up Spanish faster than anyone I've ever seen."

• • •

The leader of a national journalism association called the next morning. *The Green News-Item* had won a prestigious national journalism award to be presented in the fall in Washington, D.C.

"You and your staff exemplify the spirit of a small-town newspaper," the man from the journalism society said. "This award points to excellence on every level."

I reached down to scratch the remnants of my redbug bites.

"You can't begin to know how excellent they have been," I murmured.

18

Benny Fish and his wife, Marguerite, ran into the ditch after a low-flying buzzard was spooked off of its meal in the middle of the road and struck their vehicle's windshield. Benny suffered a broken nose when the air bag deployed. Marguerite, who was shaken up but not injured, said, "All I could say was, 'Benny, bird, bird, bird!' Then it hit us." Benny said it looked like "a bloody pillow fight" and added that "those airbags hurt."
—The Green News-Item

"Creeeeeepy," Tammy said.

She made the word sound like a door opening into a haunted house.

Wearing a sleeveless cotton shift and clunky turquoise plastic bracelets on both of her very tanned arms, she plopped down in the chair across from my desk and opened a Hershey bar.

"That was just plain weird."

I laid down my pencil and tried not to roll my eyes, shaking my head when she offered me a bite.

"I can make more sense out of this spreadsheet than I can out of you," I said. "What in the world are you talking about?"

"Get ready for a doozy of a day. The first call was one for the books."

Tammy had a theory that we could tell how an *Item* day would go by our first call. If it was a complaint or a conspiracy theory from "one of our crazies," she would immediately dig a candy bar out of her tote bag and march through the building, eating it and telling anyone she ran into to "get ready."

"We got a strange message asking if we'd accept a collect call from Major Wilson in jail. The entire thing was recorded except for where he stuck his name in. That was his voice. I'd know it anywhere."

I picked up the rectangular pink eraser that I used frequently when working on our budget and fidgeted with it. "What'd you say?"

"I said no, of course. Not only no, but heck no!"

"I wonder what he wanted? That's the first time we've heard from him since he went to jail after the fires."

"Maybe he heard Alex left and called to say hallelujah. He always said that snotty reporter ruined his life."

"Discriminating against African American homebuyers and covering up arson ruined his life. Like every other crooked politician, he wanted to shoot the messenger when it was his own fault."

"You don't think he's stirring up trouble again, do you?"

"Nothing that man could do would shock me. If

252

he calls back, take the call, and let's see what he's up to. I'd rather face him than run away."

"Are you sure?" Tammy asked. "Those calls from jail are super expensive."

My eyes widened. "How in the world would you know that?"

"It's a long story." She stood and walked to the door, peeling back the foil to finish her candy.

"Don't overdo it on the tanning bed," I said. "That's not good for you."

She looked down at her arms. "I want to look good in my bikini."

"You'll look beautiful, unless you keep this up. Then you're going to look like that actor with the orange skin."

Major Wilson called from the white-collar prison in Texas the next morning, and Tammy rushed in with an unwrapped Reese's Peanut Butter Cup.

"It's him, it's him. He's on line one. Pick it up quick. That's costing us at least five bucks a minute."

She started to sit down, stopped halfway, and looked at me, eyebrows raised. I shrugged, and she sank into the chair. I figured it couldn't hurt for her to listen and wanted to keep nothing from the staff. I thought the arson charges against Mr. Sepulvado last year might have been dropped sooner if I had leaned on the staff more to solve the mystery of the fires.

"You're a mighty hard woman to do a favor for," Major Wilson's voice said. "It isn't like I can ask my secretary to pick up the phone and place a call for me anytime I want."

"I can see that prison hasn't mellowed you."

"I can tell that marriage hasn't softened you. I figured Coach Craig would have a tough time corralling you." It almost sounded like he was laughing, but the phone clicked every few seconds, so I couldn't tell.

"Sir," I said, knowing it irritated him when I called him that, "as much am I'm enjoying our chat, it's costing a small fortune. While you may have money stashed away, the *Item* certainly does not."

"By the time I finish paying my fines, I won't have a cent to my name, but I'm calling to offer you something I do have. My sister tells me you need a place to live."

"Your sister? I didn't realize you and Eva were in touch."

"She's more thoughtful about accepting my calls than you are, Ms. Craig. She and Dub have even made it over here to see me a time or two. They brought that Mexican fellow last time. Part of my re-hab-i-li-ta-tion." He dragged the word out, almost as if testing its sound.

"Is that what this call is about? Because I've moved on from all of that." That was a lie. I resented Major Wilson and the way he used his political power to hurt poor people, and I was not sorry at all that Chuck McCuller had died. I was trying to make up my mind about Dub, figuring if Eva liked him, he must have good traits. He had taken the produce man in.

"I have a travel trailer out at my deer lease," Major said. "You and your husband are welcome to use it till you find a place."

"I'd think you'd be happy to see me homeless," I said. "Why would you offer me a place to live?"

"I like that family you married into, and I'm trying to get my life back in order. Although you sure don't make it easy."

"And where is this camper?" I was still skeptical.

"It's in the woods, behind where Old Mr. and Mrs. Craig lived."

While I tried to process what he was saying, Tammy tapped her watch and made a dollar sign in the air with her finger. She seemed to have forgotten her candy bar.

"That's a little too far out of town for us," I said, finally. "Thanks for the offer, though."

"I'm not offering it to you out there. I expect you to move it over to Aunt Helen's land."

"Oh. I'll mention it to Chris, but I think we're looking for something a little more permanent."

"If you change your mind, let Eva know. She has the key."

"While I have you on the phone," I said, "could

I ask you a couple of questions for the paper?"

"I'd love to publicize what life in jail is like," he said, "but it's time for my shift in the laundry room." The sound of the receiver slamming down was none too gentle, and a recording came on to explain how the call would be billed.

"That was creepy," I said to Tammy. "He offered to let Chris and me live in his hunting camper. Can you imagine anything worse?"

Chris liked the idea.

"It's an answered prayer," he said.

My nightmare was his answered prayer?

"It'll be a mess." I swatted a mosquito as we sat in the swing at the house place. I had met Chris there after work with dinner from the Cotton Boll in a Styrofoam container. "And we'd have to get it moved."

"My dad can move it," he said, cutting a piece of meat loaf as he spoke. "His truck has a bigger engine than mine."

"If we're going to do that, we might as well stay at the Lakeside. We have someone to clean up, and it's handy."

"A kitchen!" He was more excited than I had seen him since our disastrous house-hunting expedition. "We'll have a kitchen. And a yard."

His eyes lit up.

"We can get the dogs back. Let's at least look at it."

"It's almost dark, and we don't have the key. Can't we wait till tomorrow?"

"I'm dumbfounded that we haven't thought of this before. That goes to show how overloaded our brains are."

"Maybe we haven't thought of it because it's not a very good idea," I said. "Moving into a camper right as school's about to start?"

"Lois, honey." His tone of voice signaled I had lost this argument. "It's not ideal, but I can't live in that motel room through football season. It's either this or move in with my folks, now that they've got most of their repairs done." He raised his eyebrows.

"I guess a travel trailer wouldn't be too bad. Couldn't we rent one from a dealer?"

"Major's is free," he said. "Any money we save can go on our new place."

The sun was low over Chris's catfish pond across the road, a bright red cardinal sat on a branch by a small clump of Spanish moss illuminated by the evening light.

"It would be nice to be back out on Route Two," I said.

Chris took the same route to Dub's deer lease that we had taken to his grandparents' home.

"While we're out this way, let's stop and take another look at the old place," I said. "It's such a beautiful evening."

"I thought you vowed never to set foot on this property again after the redbug-and-poison-ivy assault," he said, turning down the overgrown road.

"Insect repellent." I opened the glove box of his truck. "I came prepared this time."

The house looked even more striking at sunset than it had the afternoon we had been there before. "It has dignity," I said. "They don't make houses like this any more."

"Not in our price range, they don't. I wish my family had taken better care of it."

"I wondered about that when we were here before. Why didn't you?"

"My parents' generation didn't like old stuff. They wanted brick and carpet and modern conveniences—which, I admit, do have their benefits. My brothers and I weren't interested in this old place once Grandma and Grandpa died, and it slowly deteriorated."

"If it weren't so far out here—"

"I didn't realize until we came out here what bad shape it's in. I suppose it's been vacant close to fifteen years."

"It's in fairly good shape to have been neglected that long."

"Daddy's a little sentimental about it," Chris said. "He comes out here and bush hogs the yard every now and then, keeps the roof patched, that sort of thing. He stores hay in the barn back there.

I am pretty sure that he hoped one of us boys would live here one day."

He looked at his watch and then at the sun, now almost totally down. "We'd better get going or it'll be too dark to see Dub's place."

He took a left out of the drive onto the narrow road and then another left, winding back in dense woods.

"How in the world do you know how to find this place?" I asked. We bumped up and down, dust whirling around on the still August night.

"When I was a teenager, I explored every inch of this land. The worst trouble I ever got into with Daddy was out by Major's place. Me and my buddies decided we'd camp out and do a little partying. I should have known I couldn't buy a case of beer in Green without someone telling on me."

"A case of beer?"

"They were tall boys, too. By the time Daddy found us, we were puking our guts out. Put me off drinking altogether."

"Sounds lovely." I grew increasingly uneasy as we pulled down the dirt road. The night sounds of crickets and tree frogs and cicadas were so loud we could easily hear them with the windows up and the air conditioner blasting on high.

The sun was completely down, and the thick woods moved us from twilight to dark within minutes. Chris turned on his headlights.

"Maybe we should come back tomorrow," I said.

"We're almost there. Wonder what that light is over there?"

In the distance a weak light flickered.

"It looks like a lantern," I said. "This is creeping me out."

"Probably high school kids. A last hurrah before school starts."

We rounded a small bend, and there sat the travel trailer, the door standing open.

"So much for needing a key," Chris said. "Looks like someone beat us to it."

"Let's go back."

"You stay here," Chris said, fishing around under his seat. "I know I have my Q-Beam here somewhere." He pulled out a big light and plugged it into the cigarette lighter. "You shine it, and I'll take a look."

"Be careful."

"Don't be a scaredy-cat. I'll protect you."

I practically held my breath when he stepped inside the trailer. An armadillo waddled out of the woods looking like a miniature dinosaur, and as I shone the light, three cute babies tagged behind their ugly mother. As I watched them cross the grassy patch in front of the truck, I noticed a cigarette butt, still glowing. I turned the headlights on, got out of the truck and looked closer. It was smoldering.

Nervous, I climbed back in the truck and locked my door, which was silly since my window was down. "Chris?" I yelled. "Don't you think we'd better get going?"

I turned the spotlight into the woods but didn't see a trace of a human being. Chris was probably right. Silly kids, probably ran off when they heard us.

While I scanned the woods, Chris jerked the truck door open and slammed the vehicle in reverse scarcely before he was in his seat.

"Turn the light off," he said.

"The place look that bad?" I tried to cover my fear with a joke.

"It looks decent enough, considering someone's using it for a meth lab."

"So by the time the sheriff's guys arrived," Linda said the next morning, "everything was cleared out."

"You have excellent sources," I said. "How could you already know that?"

"Police chief's secretary. I take her a cup of gourmet coffee from the doughnut shop on my way to work. Gets my day off to a good start."

"So what else did she tell you?"

"She said the ne'er-do-wells, as she calls them, probably knew Major Wilson was out of commission and made themselves at home. You and Chris must have showed up right as they were getting down to their nightly business."

"The sheriff didn't find anything to indicate who it was?"

"Nothing. It was clean as a whistle, which should make you happy."

"Why would that make me happy?"

"Because they're hauling the camper over to your land this afternoon. It should be ready for you to move in by the time you get off work."

"You're joking, right?"

"You know I never joke. With you living in it, no drug dealers will be able to set up shop there." She looked at her reporter's notebook. "And a quote from Doug's secretary: 'He called that good-looking coach and got the A-OK.'"

The little travel trailer looked right at home nestled in the trees near the back of our yard.

"It's kind of cute, but why'd they put it way back there?" I asked Chris as we pulled into the driveway.

"I asked them to leave room for our building project, whatever that turns out to be. I figure we can do dirt work, trim trees, that sort of thing. We can get the electricity turned on by the end of the week and be set to move in by Saturday."

"I'm glad we don't have to stay here tonight. You've got to admit it's weird to live in a place owned by Major Wilson and previously used as a drug lab."

"After these past few months, nothing seems weird to me anymore," Chris said, pushing open the door.

"Do we need to do an exorcism?" I stepped in.

"Lois, don't be rude. It was big of Major to do this, and I promise you're going to like it once we get settled."

As usual, Chris was right.

By the end of the weekend, we had scrubbed and scoured and gotten rid of years of hunting-camp odors and any germs left by ill-intentioned drug fiends.

Wayne, the sheriff's deputy who had served papers a year ago for the McCuller lawsuit against the newspaper, stopped by with Andy, the drug dog, to reassure me that there wasn't a trace of evidence left. I assumed by the German shepherd's demeanor that Wayne was right.

As the squad car backed out of the driveway, Wayne stuck his head out and hollered, "My wife said to tell you she'd be by before dark with a dewberry cobbler."

One person after another showed up to help us settle in, from Bud and Anna Grace bringing a homemade pound cake to Iris Jo and Stan, who brought new sheets and towels, and Linda, who had a box of everyday dishes and pots and pans. "Mom and Dad like it at the nursing home, so they don't need these now," she said.

"Don't you need them?" I asked.

"I've got more of their things than I'll ever be able to use."

Rose came by with a green McCoy vase and a primitive painted table with a place for books underneath. "It's small enough to fit and will give the place a homey look."

Estelle and Hugh brought a home-cooked lunch, all four dogs, and materials for a fence. Molly and half of the football team showed up to help build it.

"That was Anthony's idea," she said. "He thinks a lot of Coach."

Mannix, Markey, and Kramer rolled in the grass as though long deprived of such joy, and Holly Beth, carried inside by Molly, immediately climbed up on the bed and laid down on one of the new pillows.

Pastor Jean, Maria, and the boys delivered two hanging baskets filled with impatiens. "You'll have to keep them watered good this time of year," Jean said, "but they'll add a touch of color."

Maria studied the camper closely, walking around back, getting down on her knees to see how the steps were attached and looking at the blocks that had been placed under the wheels.

"They're moving her trailer next week to that land around the corner," Jean said. "She's concerned about how that will work. I don't think she's ever seen a mobile home moved before."

"Obviously she hasn't driven up Interstate 49

very often. Every time I've been to Shreveport I've been practically run off the road by those wide loads."

"Those homes get bigger and bigger, don't they? When you have time, Maria needs you to take care of the paperwork," the pastor said. "Don and I are helping her with the note, and the owners were easy to deal with."

"What sort of paperwork?" Chris asked.

"Note?" I said at the same time.

"Since the property's yours," she said, "you'll have to sign off on the deal with the state. They were very fair with the church, and I think you'll be happy with what you're getting. The highway department pays to move the trailer, too, which helps."

"But we gave the land to Maria, along with the mobile home," I said. "That money belongs to her."

Jean clapped her hands together. "In all of the confusion at the courthouse after the storm," she said, "that must not have been properly filed. Are you sure you want to do that, given all that's happened? Don't you need the money for your new place?"

"Yes." Chris looked at me. "We could use the money for our new place. But we're sure we want Maria to have it."

"Absolutely," I said.

19

Wild hogs are damaging fields and wooded areas, according to state official Tim Robinson, and should be approached with caution. "They are being seen in high numbers and can be quite aggressive. A Bouef Parish hunter sent me a game-camera shot of a dozen feeding near his deer stand, and a driver reported three crossing the road near the Route Two crossroads. Hunting of the hogs is regulated, so we've got us," and I quote, "a Catch-29 situation."
—The Green News-Item

Tammy sashayed into the paper glowing after her honeymoon. She gushed about the white sand on the beach and "watermelons carved into baskets and huge ice sculptures shaped like dolphins."

"Did you know on a cruise they fold your towels in the shapes of animals? And you can get pizza until two in the morning? We had dinner with people we didn't know, and I fit in good except when I snorted a bean sprout up my nose."

Her souvenir gift to us was a wooden plaque to hang outside our travel trailer, "like all the campers in Florida have." "The Craig's" was burned into it, along with a figure of a dog.

"I know that apostrophe doesn't belong there," she said, "but I didn't have the heart to get them to change it."

I couldn't get over how happy I was to see her.

"We stopped in Georgia and saw Katy," she said. "Her dorm room is so cute. She's got it all done in Georgia colors—red, black, and gray— almost like our wedding! Alex texted her three times while we were having lunch. I think they're getting serious."

"They're way too young to be serious," I said.

"Spoken like a woman who got married when she was thirty-eight."

"I'm afraid to ask, but is her dorm room bigger than our camper?"

"I haven't seen the notorious meth lab yet, but I'd say they're roughly the same size. It's a twenty-four-footer, right?"

"Something like that. Why don't you come for a visit, and I'll give you a tour. It'll take about two minutes, tops."

"Walt has a golf tournament this weekend for his law firm. Maybe I'll come Saturday."

"Perfect," I said, relieved. With Katy at college, Iris and Stan working on their building project, Chris consumed with football, and Kevin overwhelmed by patients, I felt a tad lonely. When I went into the paper on Saturdays, I kept expecting to see Tom sitting at his desk, listening to the police radio and working a crossword puzzle.

• • •

On Friday night after the Rabbits narrowly lost to a team from West Monroe, Chris flopped onto the bed, bumping his head on the fake wood headboard. Aggravated, he grabbed a throw pillow and, well, threw it, causing Holly Beth to jump down and run over to where I sat on a bench that doubled as a dining room chair.

"I must be a bad influence on you," I said, picking up the dog and moving into what might loosely be called a bedroom. "The old Chris Craig would have never thrown something. What's wrong?"

With both hands behind his head, he stretched out on the bed, his feet almost hanging off.

"Number one, the Rabbits lost tonight because Anthony Cox acted like he had never seen a football before. Number two, Asa has toys bigger than this camper. Number three, I don't know how in the heck I'm going to keep the food delivery program going for the rest of the school year."

I snuggled up next to him. Holly made a few circles and settled down right between us. I could have sworn she gave a sigh of pleasure as she drifted off to sleep.

"That's quite a list. What can I do?"

"You already do too much. You're running the paper with a skeleton crew and eking out a profit. You've jumped back in to Kids' Camp on Wednesdays, and you're on the building committee at church."

"That's only because I'm bossy. When they said metal building, I stuck my nose in. The brick front's going to help, though, and the steeple."

"I need to start a building committee for me and you," he said. "This camper is better than a motel room, but it's getting old in a hurry."

"What if I take over your food deliveries for a while? And why don't we postpone house talk until after football season? I'm happy to be back out on Route Two, to have the dogs back." I stroked Holly. "Every morning I sit out in the swing and am thankful we're alive, and that I have you. It could be much worse."

Chris was silent, and I turned my head to look at him. He was sound asleep.

Saturday, after breakfast with his parents, I hatched a plan and presented it to him as though it were a fait accompli.

"I'll do the food delivery program today while you meet with the other coaches," I said. "Go out for a hamburger with your buddies afterwards. Relax a little."

"It's not safe for you to be alone out there. A few of the places are isolated, and Doug says those meth dealers aren't to be taken lightly."

"Tammy's coming over later. I'll get her to go with me."

"That's a comforting thought."

"She can be downright scary, and you know it."

I struck a Tammy pose, both hands on my hips, pretending to chew gum, which she did ninety percent of the time. "I'd as soon kick a meth dealer in the teeth as look at him," I said, doing my best imitation.

"Is that supposed to be me?" Tammy asked, peering in the top of the aluminum door.

"Busted," I said as she walked in. "How'd I do?"

"You've got to work on what Walt calls the Tammy Twang. He says it's the cutest thing he's ever heard."

"How was the honeymoon?" Chris asked.

"Like living in a movie. You should try one of your own sometime."

A worm of regret crawled through me. For a second, I could see Chris and me sitting on our private deck in Montana, but I pushed the picture down.

"Thanks for the sign," Chris said.

"I noticed you fixed it," Tammy said, twirling her ponytail, her dark hair streaked with blonde highlights. "Pretty clever to turn the apostrophe into a daisy."

"Daddy did that," Chris said. "He was happy to have an excuse to use his Dremel tool."

"I'm sorry," I said. "I couldn't in good conscience have a display of bad grammar at the entrance to my home."

"Nice home," she said. "You've done wonders with the place. When are you moving?"

Chris and I exchanged the look that I now thought of as our married look.

"We're thinking of clearing this lot and building a house or getting one of those package deals. What do you think?" I said.

"I told Iris Jo you'd never leave Route Two," Tammy said. "This piece of land was made for you. I'm sorry you don't have your old house back. I suppose certain wounds from the tornado will never heal."

One of the things that intrigued me about Tammy was that she could seem as breezy as a coed at a sorority party one minute and as deep as Pastor Jean at others.

"Speaking of tornado wounds," I said, "how about giving me a hand with food delivery today? Chris has too much on his plate, no pun intended, and I told him we could run his route."

"That sounds fun."

"I wouldn't exactly call it fun," Chris said, "but it's interesting. Just be careful. Don't take any silly chances."

Tammy volunteered to drive the big SUV that Walt had bought her after they got engaged "to keep me safe on the highway," and we headed to downtown to load up on boxes of staples.

"Today we have frozen turkeys, too," Pastor Mali said, as he checked our list of recipients and loaded the food into the back of the vehicle.

• • •

Driving into the country, we visited with sweet little old ladies who practically wept over the food, and grouchy old men who tried to act as if they were taking it as a favor. I read Chris's map and mostly got us to the right roads, occasionally leading us into a dead end.

We approached Maria's trailer, now parked on an acre of land across the road from one of Chris's catfish farms. Big trees shaded it, and it had been spared the plopped-down look that many mobile homes in rural Bouef Parish had.

"What the tornado couldn't accomplish, the government did," I said. "Moved, lock, stock, and barrel in less than a week. It's surprising how fast officials can work when they want something."

"Where'd that porch come from?" Tammy asked.

No wonder the trailer looked so settled.

"I don't know. It wasn't there a few days ago. Neither were those flower beds."

"I think she has company." Tammy pulled into the long rutted drive. "Unless she got a fancy black pickup while I was on that cruise."

"Maybe we should come back later," I said.

"Chicken. You're just saying that because you know that's Dub McCuller's truck. You can't keep running from him forever."

"Who says I'm running from him?"

"I saw you at the town meeting, Lois. I even saw

you cross the street downtown the other day to avoid him as he came out of Eva's store."

"I can't make a move in this town . . ." I muttered. "OK, let's get the box unloaded and get out of here."

Maria answered the door with a big smile and invited us in. Dub and Mr. Sepulvado stood as we entered, and Joe insisted on taking the box.

"I've got it," I said. "I'm sure you shouldn't be lifting yet."

"I'm all healed," he said, looking younger than I remembered. "I'm ready to plant my fall garden. Maria's going to let me use part of her land."

The question must have shown on my face.

"We met at the Spanish service at Grace Chapel," the young mother said. "Joe and Mr. Dub have been a godsend in helping me and the boys settle here. Doesn't their porch look fantastic?" Her Spanish intonation gave the word "fantastic" a poetic sound.

"You built that?" I turned to Dub, astonished.

"Joe was the brains behind the operation," Dub said. "I was the hired hand." He looked every bit the carpenter in a pair of worn jeans and a chambray shirt that looked like it had been through the washer a hundred times.

Mr. Sepulvado looked as though he didn't understand, and Dub spoke to him in Spanish. Both men chuckled.

"*Loco*," Joe said, pointing to Dub.

We all laughed, although I wasn't quite sure why.

"We'd better get going." I all but shoved Tammy out the door.

"First see what the boys have," Maria said, proudly pointing out the back window to a nice-sized above-ground pool.

"That was Eva's idea," Dub said. "She said a sprinkler's fun, but those boys need a pool."

"That seems like a storybook," Tammy said as we pulled out. "You and Chris not only saved her life, you changed it forever."

"It's all Chris. He understands that 'love your neighbor' stuff much better than I do."

"You seem to be a fast learner. Where to next?"

For two more hours we wound through dusty roads, each stop seeming more desperate than the last. While the town of Green had plenty of poverty, the rural areas were something else altogether. The most overt signs of tornado damage had been fixed, but under-the-surface hurt ran deep, and many of the places we visited today had been a wreck before the storm blew through.

"So much for fairy tales," I said.

"It's hard to believe people live like this," Tammy said. "These places are worse than the countries we stopped at on our cruise. I thought the U.S. was supposed to be better than everybody else."

"Wait till you see our next stop. It's close to where we found Joe Sepulvado. Anthony, the football player that Molly hangs out with, lives here."

"The one who blew the game last night?"

I looked at her, taken aback.

"I was taking pictures. I wanted to get them online before the Monroe paper did."

"That's the guy. Chris said his head wasn't in the game last night." I motioned at the house. "This is it."

"Look at that pump and outhouse," Tammy said. "This place doesn't even have running water."

"Chris tried to get them a government trailer, but he couldn't convince the man who lives with Anthony's mother."

"Why wouldn't he rather live in a nice trailer than this dump?"

"Meth. The sheriff's department thinks he may be one of those with a meth lab or two in the woods. They couldn't find it before the storm and they haven't had time to fool with it since."

"Some children don't get a break." Her tone told me she had been one of those children. No wonder she seldom talked about her childhood.

When we drove up, Anthony sauntered out, while the little girl rushed at the truck. The baby was not with them.

"The applesauce was good," the little girl said, peering into the truck. "It's been a long time since we've had applesauce."

"We're not supposed to take any more food," the teen said. "Mama's boyfriend said it isn't right, you coming down here like we're a charity case."

The little girl's bottom lip trembled, and my heart felt as though it were ripping in two.

"Is your mother home?" I asked, earning a quick look from Tammy, who hopped out of the SUV ahead of me.

By the time we reached the sagging front porch, a young African American woman stood in the door, the baby on her hip.

"Ma'am, we're from Grace Chapel, down the road," I said. "The church is delivering food all over the area. I don't know if you've met Pastor Jean, but she'll have our hide if we don't leave this food here."

"Carry it in the house," the woman said to Anthony, and walked away without another word.

Tammy and I got in the truck, and I waved to the little girl who held a teddy bear I had slipped her.

"Have our hide?" Tammy said to me. "That didn't sound like you at all."

"My mother-in-law. Estelle is going to have Hugh's hide over one thing or another all the time."

"Good job," Tammy said, the SUV jarring my teeth as we headed to the main road.

Before we got to the end of the deserted road,

the biggest man I had ever seen stepped out of the edge of the woods and stood in front of the vehicle.

Tammy slammed on the brakes, the boxes in the back sliding forward with the force of cinder blocks.

"Go around him," I said.

"I can't make it through there." She nodded at the trees. "I'm not going to scratch the only new car I've ever had over a jerk with too much testosterone."

As the man approached, she reached behind the seat. "Don't tell me you have a gun," I said. "Lord, don't tell me she's about to pull a gun."

"Better than a gun." She let her window down about half way and glanced at me. "Lois Barker Craig, I know you don't like taking orders, but listen to me. Don't move. Don't say anything."

The man leaned on the window with a sneer. "I said we don't want you down here anymore," he said in a Spanish accent. "We don't want your food, and we don't want you poking your nose in our business."

I sat in silence. Tammy smiled as though they were visiting at the grocery store.

"Now get out of this fancy car, and start walking back to town, or I'm going to make you wish you had."

He came closer. "But before you go, give me

277

that purse." He reached in the window, over Tammy, who continued to lean into the back seat.

"Give him the purse, Tammy," I said through clinched teeth. I figured the statute of limitations had run out on my sitting still and being quiet.

Right then, Tammy, new bride of one of the region's most successful lawyers, slammed a baseball bat down on his hands and peeled out, a rock flying up and denting her new hood.

"I can see why Anthony's mind wasn't on football last night," she said.

I didn't say anything.

Two sheriff's cars, lights flashing and sirens blaring, flew past us on our way back to our camper.

Molly stopped by our place within an hour.

"That awful man's in jail," she said, "although I don't know how long they'll keep him. Anthony's mother hopes Coach will get them one of those tornado trailers. Do you think it's too late?"

"It's never too late, Molly."

Chris and Walt were not far behind her, Walt still wearing his golf shoes. To say they were upset with us would have been like saying World War II was a fistfight.

"If you ever do anything like that again," Chris said, holding me at arm's length as though to reassure himself that I was OK, "I'm going to . . . I don't know what I'm going to do."

"Have her hide?" Tammy said, throwing me a wink.

"Don't do anything like that again," Chris said.

"I wish I had gotten a picture of the look on Lois's face when I pulled out that baseball bat," Tammy said.

"I'm trying to figure out how you got the leverage to use the bat like that," I said.

Tammy's brand-new husband looked at Chris and threw up his hands. "Are all wives this much trouble?" Walt asked.

"I feel certain the answer to that is no," my husband said. "Let me show you what we're thinking about out here."

He headed down the steps, let the dogs out, and came back to the door to kiss me.

"You took more years off my life today than that tornado did," he said.

Tammy and I sat in the swing and watched the two men walk around the property, Chris gesturing and measuring with his long stride.

Walt nodded and smiled, took a tiny notebook out of his shirt pocket and wrote a few things, and counted off steps in another direction.

"Do you ever think about what could have been instead of what is?" Tammy asked.

My mind spun from the sight of her with that baseball bat, and I shook my head.

"I could be living in poverty out in the middle of nowhere or be married to a caveman like that guy on the road. Instead, I have plenty of food, a beautiful home, and that wonderful man."

"I could be living in a sterile little condo in Ohio, dreading another winter alone. Or I could have blown away in that house." I nodded at the lot.

"Aren't we lucky?" she asked.

"I'd say it goes well beyond luck."

20

Congratulations to Estelle and Hugh Craig who are celebrating their sixty-first wedding anniversary this week. There's no telling how many people Estelle has fed through the years, and Mr. Hugh is a friend to all. The Route Two scuttlebutt says the lovebirds are going on a fishing trip to Toledo Bend as soon as they get done babysitting their granddogs.
—The Green News-Item

"I owe you a honeymoon," Chris said.

"I owe you a house," I said.

"Let's get on with our life."

"You won't get an argument out of me. I'm more than ready."

The Rabbits were having a winning season with what looked to my amateur eyes like inspired play from Anthony Cox.

The *Item* was making a profit, advertisers slowly coming back.

Nearly six months had passed since the day we became husband and wife and Green became Before Tornado and After Tornado. B.T. and A.T.

"I talked to the principal and I'm adding three days to fall break at the end of the month," he said. "I've called the airline and the lodge. We're going to Montana."

He picked me up and swung me around the little trailer, my feet knocking over a lamp.

"Oh, Chris, I'm so ready to get out of town."

I floated into work the next morning, looking like Tammy often did these days.

"Honeymoon. Me. Chris." I said as I jumped over the swinging door in the lobby, a patented Tammy move.

Within moments, Iris Jo, Linda, and Tammy were in my office.

"We've been working on an idea," Linda said.

"Oh, I just bet you have. How much money is this going to cost me?"

"We're making a little profit," Iris Jo said.

"Very little, as I recall."

"Let's have a redo of your wedding reception," Tammy said.

"And invite the entire town," Linda said.

"On the site of the old Grace Community Chapel," Iris said.

"A tent," Tammy said. "Hold on. I'll show you." She headed for the lobby.

"I know what a tent looks like."

"You said one time you'd always wanted a party with a big white tent," Iris Jo said.

I couldn't believe she remembered that.

"I have, but I'm not sure Green's ready for a party. This town has been through so much."

"That's precisely why Green *needs* a party," Linda, the most sober person I knew, said.

"No offense, but your wedding reception was not much fun," Tammy said. "You deserve a real one, where people sit in the chairs instead of dodge them."

I laughed despite myself. "Exactly when would this party be?"

"Right before your honeymoon," Iris said. "You love fall in Louisiana almost as much as you love spring."

Oh, she was right. Fall in Green was a blend of relief from the hot days of summer and a colorful spectacle, the light shining off the rust of cypress trees on the lake, coming through the yellows of sweet gums and bringing a complete change of attitude.

"Let me think about it, and see what Chris thinks."

"You're consulting Chris before you make a decision?" Tammy said. "You really are an old married couple now."

My first call was to Marti, happily married to a preacher in the making. "Please, please, please. You and Gary come down for a few days. It'll be much better weather than your July visit last year. You can see the Craig Meth Casa. I can get you the newlywed suite at the Lakeside Motel."

Next I called Kevin. "What are you doing the last Saturday in October?"

"Taking Asa to the park?"

"How about bringing Asa to my wedding reception do-over?"

"We're there," she said.

"Want to bring Terrence?"

"Don't push your luck."

Eva was in the command center at the courthouse, now down to two hours a week.

"I could use a party," she said when I broached the subject. "May I bring Sugar Marie?"

"Of course. I'll bring Holly Beth. We'll let bygones be bygones. Bring Dub, too."

A pleased smile lit her face. "He'll be delighted."

I texted Katy. "U. Here. Last Sat. in Oct. Party. Me. Chris. Miss U."

"Can't wait. Miss U 2." She answered within a minute.

Next I tracked down Pastor Jean. "Will you say a few words?"

"Oh, Lois, I'd be honored."

Finally I caught up with Chris by phone after school.

"Our plane tickets are for that Saturday evening," he said. "We'll be cutting it close."

"For me?" I asked.

"Consider it done," he said. "I've got to run. Faculty meeting today. Getting pressure from the state since the tornado. Love you."

"Love you back."

Bud came up with the idea that pleased me most. "October's the perfect time to plant trees," he said. "Let's give every guest a tree. We lost so many of our beautiful oaks."

"I'll coordinate the food," said Anna Grace, never far from Bud these days. "As the food writer, I have a little clout."

"You're a brave soul. My last reception nearly killed you."

My in-laws were over the top about the party, spending every one of our Saturday family breakfasts discussing it with military precision.

"Then what will happen?" Estelle would ask.

"Would we have the food before or after Pastor Jean's remarks?"

"What's with those guys?" I asked Chris as we headed out. "They act like we're planning to invade a small country."

"They're probably scarred from our first reception, baby. It didn't exactly go as planned."

"Tornado season is over, right?" I asked.

"Yes, and you know what they say about lightning striking twice."

"That's not exactly the reassurance I hoped for," I said.

"I need reassurance on our house plans," Chris said. "What are you thinking?"

"That if you clear any more trees we'll be living in the middle of a field. Aren't you going a little overboard?"

"I talked to the sales guy about the prefab cottages. He says they need lots of room to get the trucks in."

My face fell. "You think that's the route we should go? Those houses have plastic that they try to make look like wood."

"I talked to that architect friend of Walt's in Shreveport. She says if we build, we'll need a larger area for a foundation. The trees had sort of grown around Helen's house."

"That's one of the things I loved about it. Like your grandparents' house. It looks like it was always there."

"We've agreed, haven't we, that the old house is too far out of town and out of our price range?"

"Yes. It's just that those old houses are . . . noble. Everything else looks bland when I remember what Aunt Helen gave me."

"Let's scrap the plastic house and build," he said. "It'll take longer, but it'll be worth it. Do you think you can live in the Meth Mobile for a year?"

"If I'm with you, I can live anywhere."

Marti wouldn't commit to the reception, a major disappointment since my brothers said they couldn't make a second trip to Green in a year.

"Can't or won't?" I asked.

"Let's say we'd rather have you and Chris come up here," the eldest said. "We don't exactly have fond memories of your new hometown."

"Seriously, Sis," my younger brother said, "it's too expensive to get our families down there for a weekend. We'd have to take the kids out of school. It's a logistics nightmare."

When Marti finally called me at the office a few days before the party, I was not surprised by her decision.

"We can't make it this weekend," Marti said.

I tried not to cry.

"Because we're here now," she said, stepping around the door with her cell phone up to her ear.

I dropped the phone and tackled her. Gary stood to the side.

"You came, you came, you came!" I screamed. "Iris, Tammy, Linda, Marti's here!"

"They set it up," Gary said, stepping around the door.

"Oh, Gary, you, too! Thank you for bringing Marti to our party."

"Bringing Marti? Wild horses couldn't have kept her away."

• • •

Saturday dawned cool and beautiful, and I awoke early, excited about the day ahead. Sitting in the swing with Holly in my lap, Chris still asleep, I thought about the spring morning of our wedding, a fresh morning, similar to this but with a different feel.

The past six months had felt endless when I was in the middle of them, but now it seemed as though they had zoomed by, the seasons changing as steadily as my life. Spring had been fresh, but fall felt . . . right. I loved being Chris's wife, and I knew we could make it through whatever storms came our way.

I left Chris a note and, with all of the dogs, walked to the church lot, the site of the party. The crew hammered and whizzed around, setting up the tent, tables, and chairs.

"The weather looking good?" I asked the foreman.

"Not a cloud in sight."

"Wind?"

"None. You picked the perfect day for a party."

"That's what I thought in March, too."

"Trust me. Even if a storm blows through, this tent isn't going anywhere."

"Don't even say that."

"What time are you starting?" a workman asked, hammering a spike into the ground.

"Eleven o'clock sharp. Wrapping up at three and going on my honeymoon."

Marti drove up in a small rented SUV as I stood there.

"You really are in Green," I said. "You had me convinced you wouldn't make it."

"So this is where you got married?"

"It has an airy feel, doesn't it?" I pointed at the slab where the church had been bulldozed. "Tammy calls it the highway of love."

"So the interchange will be over there?" Marti motioned to the corner.

"It feels different, doesn't it? It's weird with Chris's trailer moved and the parsonage turned into a construction office."

"But you have a nice buffer there," she said, "with all those trees. It's your own little corner of the world. Are you excited about building a house?"

I had known Marti for more than twenty years and knew when she was fishing. "Are you worried that I'm not happy?"

She looked startled. "You were so settled in Aunt Helen's house when Gary and I came last summer. I thought you might be having adjustment problems."

I looked around, as though someone might hear. "Don't tell Chris," I said, "but I fell in love with his grandparents' house. I haven't been able to get it out of my mind. I wish I had time to take you out there to see it."

"Why don't you move there?"

"It's a wreck and way too far out of town. When all was said and done, it wasn't practical."

"Moving to Green wasn't the most practical thing either, but look how it worked out."

"But I'm married now. My husband's a practical kind of guy."

"Men," she said with the look only a friend of decades could muster and gave me a huge hug. "Let's take you home and get you ready for the party."

Chris had left a note. "Gone to run an errand or two. Will pick Gary up. See you at the party."

"Isn't it weird how marriage changes you?" I asked. "I'm sort of disappointed Chris and I aren't getting ready together."

"Strange thing, love," Marti said. "After all those years, when we fell, we fell hard."

I slipped into the newest of Miss Barbara's original creations, a burnt-orange chiffon two-piece outfit that swirled when I moved.

"You look like an autumn leaf," Marti said. "Let's put your hair up in one of those perky topknots."

"I'll ride down to the church with you," I said. "Chris and I will have to come back here to get our suitcases before the trip."

"If I were you, I'd take my car, just in case."

"Just in case what?" My eyes got big. "There's not a storm in the forecast, is there?"

"You've got to calm down about this storm

business. Take your car in case if we have to pick anything up at the last minute, that sort of thing." She kept looking at her watch and pulling at her short blonde hair the way she did when she was nervous.

"Is everything OK with you and Gary? You're acting strange."

"It feels like your wedding day. I'm a little nerved up. Let me get dressed and let's go down to the church."

By the time we arrived, Becca and two women from Grace were setting up the flowers, simple calla lilies in cylindrical vases on every table with a branch of bright leaves from nearby trees. The contrast between the formal lily and the tree limbs was stunning.

Bud and Anna Grace arrived early and were lining the gift trees up. A row of small clay pots decorated a table over to the side, a smaller tag tied around them with ribbon.

"What are these?" I asked, picking up one to inspect.

"Acorns, waiting to become mighty oaks," Bud said.

"They're from the most beautiful trees around town." Anna Grace patted Bud on the back. "Bud planted them, and I did the tags."

I looked closer and saw that the pots were grouped according to where the acorns came from—library, Methodist church, Green High courtyard. "May your love always grow," Anna Grace had written in her spidery old script. "In honor of Lois & Chris."

"When your children have children, these will be beautiful oaks, rooted in Green," she said.

I heard Marti sniff behind me, and she handed me a tissue. "Just in case."

Hand in hand we strolled under the tent, my excitement growing by the moment. Tammy snapped setup pictures, although I didn't see Walt.

"He's probably coming later," Iris Jo said when I asked her about it.

Stan was helping set up for the music to be played by Pastor Jean's husband, Don, and Jolene, the niece of a church member. Someone was obviously going to play drums, too, although I had no idea who.

When the Mayor and Dub pulled in, Sugar Marie sailed out of the car and over to me, sniffing and then running back to Eva.

"I forgot Holly Beth," I said. "You were right, Marti. Good thing I brought my car."

"No," Marti yelled, so abruptly that I stepped back.

"Are you sure you're OK?"

"Let me get her for you. Your guests are arriving."

"She doesn't know you that well. It won't take five minutes."

I thought I saw Iris, Marti, and Pastor Jean exchange a look, but I headed for the house.

When I pulled up, I nearly screamed. Chris, Walt, and Gary were in the yard, driving wooden stakes and sticking small orange flags into the ground.

When they saw me, they jumped back, "guilty as sin," Tammy's favorite expression.

"You know it's time for the party, and you're not even dressed yet. Can't you do that when we get back from Montana?"

"Walt talked to his architect friend, and she had good ideas about where we might build the house," my sweaty husband said. "We're getting an idea of how it might look."

"Now?" I shrieked. "Now? Has anyone ever killed her husband before the honeymoon?"

"My bad," Chris said. "Why are you here anyway? Aren't you supposed to be meeting and greeting?"

"I forgot Holly. I promised Eva I'd bring her."

"I'll be right behind you," Chris said. "I'm headed to the shower right now."

He gave Walt and Gary a stricken look.

"Me, too," Tammy's husband said. "I've got my party clothes inside. Be right there."

"And me," Gary said. "Don't tell Marti, OK?"

"Remember your tie," I said with a disgusted sigh.

"Got it," Chris said, remarkably cheerful about the hated article of clothing.

I stalked back to the car with Holly Beth and drove off. When I looked in the rearview mirror, they were back to hammering the stakes.

I spotted my family immediately as I pulled back into the lot, my brothers shaking hands with the Craig men, and my sisters-in-law chatting with Jean and Iris as though they were the oldest of friends.

Tears gushed out of my eyes. No wonder Marti thought I'd need a tissue.

Our group hug lasted for minutes, and many of those around us clapped.

"Me, too, me, too," a high female squeal said, and Katy wrapped her arms around me. Although it had only been two months since I had seen her, she looked so . . . grown up.

As the hug broke up, Walt and Chris appeared, Chris wearing the new rust-colored striped tie and sticking closer to me than he had done at our wedding.

We wandered throughout the area, watching people load their plates with homemade food, ranging from Maria's chicken enchiladas to Stan's brisket to Tammy's creamed corn to Estelle's peanut-butter fudge and Mayor Eva's lemon squares, ordered from the Country Club.

The band played while the crowd visited and ate, a breeze wafting through the tent. Stan was the unknown drummer, and joined the trio to play amazingly good versions of "Mustang Sally" and "Blueberry Hill."

Jean walked to the stage, did a twirl with Don, and took the microphone.

"Surely we could not gather on this spot on this beautiful fall day without recalling words from the book of Ecclesiastes," Jean said. "There is, indeed, a time for everything. A time to plant these new trees to replace those that were uprooted. A time to weep, which we've done plenty of, and, today, a time to laugh."

A chorus of "amens" came forth.

Mr. Marcus eased his way to the front of the crowd, little Asa clinging to his hand. I glanced over to see Kevin standing by her mother . . . and Terrence. I briefly shot her a "what's up with that?" look, and she smiled and shrugged.

"Oh, Lord, our God," Marcus prayed, "we celebrate today the marriage of this man and woman who have shown their faith, their hope, and their love during these early months of their union. We ask for an outpouring of blessings upon them, and we thank you for the lives they've touched. Amen."

He handed the microphone to Mr. Sepulvado. "*Ellos me rescató*," he said. "They rescued me. They are special."

"Lois introduced me to my husband," Tammy yelled, putting fingers in her mouth to let out one of her whistles.

"And she introduced me to my wife," Walt said, planting a big kiss on Tammy.

The crowd yelled.

"Coach brought food to our house many times," Anthony said, clearing his throat as he spoke.

"He fixed my fence," one of the elderly women from the congregation said.

"Lois encouraged me when I decided to stay in Green for college," Molly said.

"And she didn't beat me up when I chose broadcast journalism," Katy shouted.

Our guests cheered more.

"They've made Route Two the kind of place anyone would want to call home," Iris Jo said, "and we're proud to call them neighbors."

At that moment the band struck up a modified version of "Sweet Home, Alabama," inserting the word Louisiana. Don directed the crowd to sing along, and the words "Sweet Home, Louisiana" rang through the air, time and again.

I scanned the crowd, some dancing, some singing, most talking; the Mayor and Dub, Kevin and Asa and Terrence, Pearl and Marcus, Iris Jo and Stan, Tammy and Walt, Katy and Molly, Linda and Rose, Marti and Gary, my brothers, and my new family, the Craigs. Holly Beth wiggled out of Eva's arms and ran to me.

My heart pounded, and I looked at the clear blue sky, the bluest I'd ever seen.

Chris squeezed my hand and looked over his

shoulder again, and I noticed Hank and Doug standing near the corner, wearing fluorescent vests and holding walkie talkies.

Doug nodded directly at Chris, and slowly the crowd started moving toward Route Two, holding hands, chattering, the band playing "Sweet Home, Louisiana" again and again. The excitement was almost palpable.

"What's going on?" I asked Chris.

Suddenly from the paved two-lane road, a huge truck came into view, creeping along, followed by another one that looked almost identical.

"Somebody's moving a house during our party?" I asked.

I looked again. It was the old Craig house, cut down the middle.

"I hope you're up for a remodeling project, Lois Barker Craig." Chris grabbed my hand and led me onto the gravel road.

The trucks painstakingly made the wide turn, the crowd lining both sides of the road, clapping, Wayne and Bud and men from the church making sure no one got in the way.

"Let's guide her on home," my husband said. We walked in front of the house, which would be pieced back together, better than ever.

Right as we got to our lot, Mannix climbed over the fence, a move I'd not seen him make since he had lost his leg in the tornado. He ran out to us and barked, a sound not heard in months. Holly leapt out of my arms and flung herself at him, and they rolled around gleefully.

I was so thrilled that I felt like joining them.

Chris and I stepped into the yard, staked off where the big old house would sit.

I looked back at my cheering friends and family.

What had Mayor Eva called it that day back in the spring?

The glory of Green.

Discussion Questions

1. During her years in Green, Lois has begun to put down roots. What has helped her be able to do this? What has held her back? Have you ever felt a yearning to put roots in one place, or have you enjoyed moving around? In what ways was your experience similar to Lois's? How was it different?

2. Lois receives a surprise suggestion from Chris Craig during chapter 1 of *The Glory of Green*. Why does his idea catch her off guard? How does the idea symbolize changes in their relationship? How does she handle the suggestion? Have you ever had a time when you had to talk about an issue with friends to find the solution? Were they helpful?

3. *The Glory of Green* includes many joys and losses for Lois and other characters. What are some of the happiest moments? What are the saddest? Was there a scene that particularly touched you? What words would you use to describe this novel?

4. In this third book in the Green series, characters react in different ways to difficult

situations. How do they deal with problems? What works best? Where do their biggest challenges occur? Do you think the people of Green rose to the occasion or ran from it? In what ways did they help one another?

5. Lois enjoys making plans for how things should unfold, but life in Green never goes quite as she plans. In what ways are her plans shaken? Have you had experiences when things did not work out as you planned? How did you handle those situations? In addition to Lois, others in Green are making plans. Are the plans of others affected by Lois? If so, how? Do you think people should try to plan more or see what unfolds as they go along? What advice would you give Lois and friends about planning?

6. The town of Green, Louisiana, is a key part of *The Glory of Green*. What are Lois's feelings about Green now that she is in her third year there? What do you like about Green? What are your concerns about Green? What part does the new highway play in the story? Would you like to visit Green? If so, who would you chat with first? How do the community correspondents for *The Green News-Item* affect your perception of Green?

7. What are some of the ways Pastor Jean and Lois interact? How does their relationship change during the book? How does Lois help Jean, and how does Jean help Lois? How might you describe Lois's spiritual life? Is her faith strong or weak? Is there someone in your life whom you lean upon for help with problems? Have you ever been asked to reciprocate with advice of your own?

8. Dub McCuller and Mayor Eva Hillburn seem to have a complex relationship in *The Glory of Green*. Why does their friendship matter to Lois? How does she handle it? Do you think she should have responded differently? Major Wilson, a person Lois does not respect, contacts her with a surprise offer. Why do you think he called her? What do you think of her conversation with him? What do you think the future holds for Major Wilson?

9. Lois and Chris continue to be troubled by poverty in the rural areas around Green. What do they do about it? Are their efforts helpful? One family, including a football player for the Green High Rabbits, lives with a variety of troubles. What are some of those? What might be done for those children? Do you

encounter people in need in your daily life? How do you respond when confronted with poverty?

10. Citizens of Green have a variety of opinions on how things should be done. What are some of their differences of opinions? What do they agree on? Do disagreements hold Green back or help it move forward? If you had been in the town meeting, what topic would you have wanted to address? What part does the staff of *The Green News-Item* play in discussions about the future? In what ways, if any, do they shine, and in what ways, if any, do they flounder? What part do members of the media play in Green's situation?

11. What is Chris Craig's role in *The Glory of Green*? In what ways is he a catalyst in Lois's life? Does she change him? How does life surprise Chris and Lois? How does this affect their relationship?

12. Many women touch Lois's life. What does she learn from them? Who has the biggest impact on her? Do you think Lois frustrates her women friends? How does Iris Jo handle her illness? In what ways does Dr. Kevin contribute to the town? What are Eva's strengths as mayor? What words would you

use to describe Tammy? What do you think Linda, learning to be a reporter after years as a secretary, wants in life?

13. Students Molly and Katy are woven throughout the book. How do they grow? What draws them together as best friends? What do they get from their relationship with Lois? What does she get from them? What do you think will happen as they mature?

14. Lois is adapting to her puppy, Holly Beth, a gift from Mayor Eva. Do you think her relationship with the dog changes her? Chris's dog, Mannix, also has a role in this story. How does Mannix affect Lois throughout the book? Have you ever had a pet that made a difference in your life? If so, how?

15. Home is very important to Lois, and she has settled happily into the old cottage Aunt Helen gave her. What disrupts her notions of home? How does she deal with the changes? What characteristics do you think she wants in a home? What does Chris want? What matters most to you about home? What makes a house or apartment the place you want to come home to?

Center Point Publishing

600 Brooks Road • PO Box 1
Thorndike ME 04986-0001 USA

(207) 568-3717

US & Canada:
1 800 929-9108
www.centerpointlargeprint.com

9/11